There I was on the rooftop of the school, looking over the side of the building as the *entire* squadron of hall monitors closed in behind me. I glanced over my shoulder, trying to estimate how much time I had before they caught me.

Ten seconds at best.

I was completely cornered without a single escape option. I leaned my head over the edge and saw the grass two stories down. There were groups of students clumped together over most of the schoolyard and parking lot, staring and pointing fingers at me. The wind picked up and blew my hair around, making my stomach queasy.

Looking to the sky, I did my best to push the dizzy feeling out of my body. If I stared at the clouds or something, maybe I could trick myself into thinking I *wasn't* on the rooftop of my school.

A small flock of flying birds caught my eye. I found myself wishing I had wings. How had my life come to this? I'm just a sixth grader in a boring school! My hobbies were video games, drawing, and blending into my surroundings! So how was it that every hall monitor was chasing after me? How was it that the principal wanted to throw me in detention for the rest of my life?

I gripped my hand around the canvas strap on my shoulder and pulled it tighter. The time capsule attached to the strap pressed against my shirt as it rose. The weight of the capsule surprised me. It was heavy – heavier than I expected, at least.

How could such a small container be the source of so much trouble?

I took a breath, listening to the footsteps of a hundred monitors circle behind me. I know, right? *A hundred* monitors for *me*. Seems like a bit of an overreaction for one kid…

But instead of being afraid, I smiled, confident that even a *hundred* of 'em couldn't stop me.

My name is Brody Valentine, and this is the story of the best *and* worst day of my entire life.

SECRET AGENT 2
6th GRADER
ICE COLD SUCKERPUNCH

BY **MARCUS EMERSON**
AND NOAH CHILD

ILLUSTRATED BY DAVID LEE

EMERSON PUBLISHING HOUSE

This one's for Kirby, Miah, Mary, and Nathan...

Text copyright © 2013 by Emerson Publishing House.
Illustrations copyright © David Lee

Emerson Publishing House

Book design by Marcus Emerson.

It started earlier that morning. I missed the bus so my dad had to drop me off at school, which actually meant that I was a little early since my bus was always late. With the extra few minutes I had to spare, my dad gave me a couple bucks so I could eat breakfast in the cafeteria before school started.

"Two dollars enough, Brody?" my dad asked through the rolled down window of his car.

"Yeah," I replied, stuffing the dollar bills into my front pocket. "It'll be fine."

My dad smiled at me. "Put that in your wallet!"

"I *will*," I said, "but my wallet is in my *locker* so I'll have to grab it from there first."

"Why don't you carry it around?" he asked.

"I don't know," I replied, trying to think of a nicer way to say that the wallet was uglier than a goat's butt. It was made of white leather and had little metal spikes that lined the outside of it. At the center of the spikes was a red "X" that my dad drew with a marker. He said it was punk rock, but I thought it looked like something a vampire would carry. "I just don't think about it after I toss it in my locker."

I saw my dad shrug his shoulders. "Well, get used to it," he said, and then he playfully added, "That's part of growing up!"

I smirked. A leather vampire wallet was part of growing up?

"Have a good day," my dad said. "Try not to break too many hearts, *Mr. Valentine*, okay?"

I hated when he joked about our last name like that. Just because it's "Valentine" didn't automatically make me smooth with the ladies. I shot him a thumbs-up and groaned. "Roger roger. Ten-four. Copy that."

My dad rolled up the window and peeled out of the parking lot. I'm not sure if it was on purpose to make me think he was cool or if it was an accident because he wasn't too great with a clutch. Anyway, it would've been embarrassing if there were any other students outside, but since I was early, there weren't. Lucky me.

I walked up to the front doors of the school and

glanced at the sign looming overhead. As a sixth grader at Buchanan School, I had walked under this sign every day since the first day of kindergarten, but never really looked at it until that moment.

The "B" at the beginning of "Buchanan" was nearly twice as big as my head. The rest of the letters were about half that size. As I studied the letters, I noticed the last "n" looked wonky, almost as if it wanted to run away. Oh well. That's what you get when you go to a school that doesn't really care for things like "maintenance."

After I stepped through the front doors, I immediately made my way toward the kitchen. I decided to skip my locker, which meant my wallet would have to stay in there for the time being. I didn't mind. The spikes made that thing uncomfortable in my back pocket anyway.

There were a couple kids in the breakfast line so I grabbed a tray and took my place behind them. As I looked over what the kitchen was serving for breakfast, I overhead some of the kids talking.

"That time capsule is getting dug up this morning, isn't it?" a boy asked.

"That's right, I forgot all about that," replied the girl he was talking to. "They're doing it right after the bell rings, aren't they?"

"Yeah," the boy said, pointing to a spot behind her. "And it's gonna get broadcast all over the school's television system."

I glanced over my shoulder looking at the television he was pointing at. Hanging from the wall was one of the large LED televisions Buchanan School used to make announcements. On the screen was a slideshow switching between images of sports games and random reminders of when a certain club was going to meet. I imagined the video of Sebastian playing on the screen and then chuckled quietly to myself.

It's only been a week since Sebastian was busted for the candy scandal, but he was already back at school. He got two days of detention for it, but since our school has a "three strikes," policy, he was still allowed to be the president of Buchanan. I guess that means he can perform two more "random acts of evil" before they decide he's not fit to be leader or something? Oh well, right? Not much I can do about it now, and actually there's not much I *want* to do about it anymore. Getting involved in the candy scandal was *more* than enough excitement for me.

It's strange to think the whole thing only took place a week ago. Sebastian was selling overpriced candy to the students of Buchanan. Most of the operation took place in the lower level of the school, which is also known as "the dungeon." I found a video of him talking about his plans and played it through the television system so everyone would know how much of a turd that kid was.

AGENT LINUS   AGENT MADDIE

But I didn't do it alone. There were two kids that got me caught up in that whole mess. A boy named Linus, and a girl named Maddie. The two claim they work for a secret agency located somewhere in the school, and after the events of last week, I don't doubt them for a second.

Did it completely change my life and flip it upside down? Nope. Mostly because nobody even knew it was happening. The only thing anyone saw was a video that started playing by itself at the end of the day. I'm pretty alright with that though. I'm a bit of a loner at this school – not cool, not *un*cool, but somewhere in the middle, which makes me more invisible than you'd think.

Once sixth grade started, everyone began separating into different groups while I sort of stayed in my own little world. There are other kids I talk to now and again, but I seriously doubt they'd know my name if you asked them. It's cool though. It doesn't bother me if I don't think about it.

Anyway, right after that mess with Sebastian ended, Linus handed me a business card that had an inkblot of a raven with the numbers 17 and 4 in roman numerals on it. He said if I was interested in what they were offering, I could find them there, which meant if I wanted to join their secret agency, I would have to solve the puzzle on the card.

I haven't tried to figure out the clue on the business card yet, but it's still in my wallet. I wanted to take it easy before deciding whether or not to follow through. It was a crazy and exhausting thrill ride that I couldn't say I'd like to experience ever again.

…but it doesn't seem to matter where I *hide* from trouble because trouble is super good at *finding* me.

After grabbing an orange juice and a biscuit, I

stepped into the cafeteria and scanned the room for a seat. Even though it was early, there were still plenty of students who were already at school. I guess a few of them have clubs or morning basketball practice they have to be at. I hope to have an ounce or two of athletic ability someday so I could be one of those kids at practice, but I think I need to fill out my scrawny little body first or I'll likely break a bone.

The cafeteria was a mess of confusion as I walked down an aisle. Metal curtain rods were scattered at various parts of the room and had black sheets draped over them. It almost looked like a crudely created maze. How anyone was able to find a spot was beyond me because I seriously almost forgot where I was as I peeked down every aisle. At one point, I thought I found the end of the maze, but instead I found myself back in the lobby of the school.

"Really?" I grunted, spinning in place with my tray in hand. I headed back to try and find a seat. After a few more minutes of frustration, I found my way out of the maze of sheets and stood in front of the open floor of the cafeteria.

Finally, I saw an empty table near the back that looked like a great spot for a quiet breakfast alone.

Setting my tray down, I took a seat on the bench. The table I chose was right next to the stage. And then I saw the reason for all the draped sheets. The drama club was using those sheets as a set for one of their productions.

I had totally forgotten about the play until I saw the rest of the stage. Watching from my spot, I saw a bunch of students hard at work moving random items around on the stage, preparing for a drama they were supposed to put on for the rest of the sixth grade class during lunch. It was about a football team that had to learn how to accept a werewolf as one of their teammates. Funny, right? Some kid named Brayden was in charge of it. Some say he's a werewolf fanboy, while others say he's just weird. Either way, the drama meant missing a few classes so I was all for it.

After scarfing down my biscuit, I glanced at the clock. There were only a few minutes left until homeroom, so I snatched my backpack off the floor and hopped into the lobby.

The sea of students was already splashing violently in the hallways of the school. I squeezed the straps of my backpack, kept my head down, and dove in, determined to make it to homeroom without drowning.

Luckily my class was just down the hall so all I had to do was basically flow with the blob of students until my door was in view. After getting lurched a few times by the current, I was able to slip safely into my classroom.

Just as I took my seat, I heard the bell ring. School had officially started.

Instantly, the television at the front of the room flickered on. It took a minute before anyone even noticed, but the hushed whispers from students slowly silenced as the school news started playing janky intro music.

I sighed, listening to the lead guitar and obvious electric drum machine play behind a cheesy jingle written by one of the younger gym teachers in the school. Once the music finished with a drum solo, some blue and white graphics appeared onscreen as the video zoomed in on a sixth grade reporter.

EARLY WORM NEWS REPORT
DEBBIE JOHNSON

"Good morning, Buchanan School," said the girl reporter as she held a microphone in front of her face. "My name is Debbie Johnson, and you're watching The Early Worm News Report."

I sunk into my desk and leaned back, settling in for a lame news update about some kind of time capsule.

Debbie continued as the camera followed her, shaking slightly from the cameraman. "As most of you

11

already know, today is the day that Mrs. Olsen's science class has decided to dig up the time capsule that was buried back in 1999."

Was 1999 considered a long time ago? I guess it *was* before any sixth grader was born.

"And we're here live so you won't miss a second of it!" Debbie said, smiling. "Many years ago, back in the last *century*, Mrs. Olsen's science class filled a plastic tube with things that were considered popular and valuable to them."

One of the students off camera shouted. "The *real* news story is that Mrs. Olsen is old enough that she was still a teacher! That was like, last millennia or whatever!"

A bunch of kids in my homeroom class laughed.

Debbie laughed too, but ignored the comment as she walked through the schoolyard. "A time capsule, for those of you who don't know, is a container filled with items that are considered important during the year it was buried – items that tell the story of what life was like long ago. And a capsule from the year 1999 is sure to have some *super* old school stuff, such as VHS tapes or even CDs. Did you know if kids wanted to listen to music back then, they'd have to play something called a 'compact disc' or 'CD,' which was similar to a DVD, but wasn't able to play movies or anything. And what's worse is that those CDs only held about 15 songs and could only be played in a CD player!"

Some chuckling came from the front of the room. I have to admit that I laughed a little too. Debbie was poking fun at the idea that CDs were something we didn't understand.

Finally, Debbie reached the spot where Mrs. Olsen's science class had started digging. It was on the other side of the school, near the garbage bin that was next to the monkey bars. If you remember, that's where Linus had left his journal for Maddie and me to find last week. I'm *sure* it was just a coincidence.

Debbie turned back to the camera and put on her game face. "As you can see behind me, the digging has already started. Mrs. Olsen's entire first period science class is on the sidelines, waiting with teeth clenched as more of the dirt is moved away. Mrs. Olsen is here at the dig site along with Principal Davis and Coach Cooper," Debbie said as she moved toward Mrs. Olsen. Pointing the microphone at the science teacher's face, Debbie spoke. "Do you have anything to say to our viewers?"

Mrs. Olsen curled her lip. "I *heard* that joke about my age," she snipped.

Debbie stumbled over her words. "Uh, um, I uh… no no no. That wasn't *me*. That was some other student that shouted over me."

"Mm hmm," Mrs. Olsen hummed with her lips pressed together. "We'll see when I review the footage. That's fine, can we just start over? Walk up to me again and ask that same question."

Debbie looked confused. "Mrs. Olsen, we're *live* on air *right now*."

Mrs. Olsen's face immediately flushed with rage,

but she did her best to keep it in check. Through her teeth, she sneered. "Would've been nice of you to say that to *begin* with," she whispered. The rage disappeared from her face as her mouth cracked a smile. "But yes, Debbie, we're all very excited to see what the time capsule from 1999 carries within it."

"You're so old that you forgot, right?" Debbie joked.

Mrs. Olsen bit her lip. It was obvious that she was about to explode, especially since the camera was slowly zooming in on the throbbing blood vessel on her forehead. "Funny," she said. "Just *wait* till you're in class, young lady."

All of a sudden the camera jerked to the side. There were shouts coming from the dig site, but because the video was shaking so violently, it was impossible to tell what was happening. It looked like a horror movie. The screams only made it *more* scary.

Mrs. Olsen's voice cut through the blurry footage. "What do you mean there's nothing there? That's impossible! The capsule should be there! What do you mean 'you think I'm *too old* to remember?'"

The image on the television was a green blur along with the heavy breathing of the cameraman. The green was probably from the grass. The heavy breathing was probably because he was chubby.

"It's not here anymore!" shouted a girl's voice from the television.

Debbie's voice answered. "What do you mean

'anymore?'"

At last, the camera focused in on the dig site. Most of Mrs. Olsen's science class was huddled around the massive hole they had dug.

The girl continued to speak as the camera focused on her hand pointing at the hole. "You can tell that something *used* to be buried there! See how the shape of the dirt looks like something had been pressed into it for several years? That must be from the time capsule, but it's clearly not there anymore! It's *missing!*"

The camera continued to switch between blurry and sharp as the image zoomed in closer to a dirty object at the bottom of the pit. I had to look away from the screen to keep from getting motion sickness. A boy hopped into the hole and started reaching for it.

Debbie spoke as the camera continued to go in and out of focus. "Hold on one second, viewers! It looks as though the time capsule has gone missing! *Stolen* from the dig site before anyone even dug it up!"

Everyone in my homeroom was suddenly interested, leaning forward in their desks. Even *I* was on the edge of my seat, shocked that someone would do such a terrible thing.

On the screen, the camera was still focused on the boy in the pit, studying the dirt covered object.

"What's that you have there?" Debbie asked, pointing her microphone at the middle of the pit.

The boy spoke loudly as he brushed off the object. "I'm not sure exactly. It looks like... like a *wallet* or something!"

Oh, buuuurn! The thief forgot their wallet at the scene of the crime! *Classic* dumb criminal mistake! I leaned back, put my hands behind my head, and waited for the news reporter to open the wallet and solve the crime already.

Debbie snatched the wallet out of the boy's hands and held it in front of the camera. The video was still shaky and blurry, but some of the features of the wallet were pretty clear. Most of the dirt had been scraped off and revealed that the leather was white.

Weird, I thought. Someone else besides me owns a white leather wallet? I shook my head, feeling sorry for the kid who owned the wallet because he was about to get called out on live television.

I watched the screen and noticed that the wallet in Debbie's hands had other similarities to my own wallet, which was in my locker. Along the edges were little spikes embedded into the leather, and at the center of the those spikes was… a red letter "X" that was drawn with a *marker*.

Uh-oh…

My heart sank into my butt as I stared at the screen. There had to be *two* of these punk rock vampire wallets in the world, right? Mine couldn't have been the *only* one in existence!

I watched the blurry video of Debbie's face as she fumbled about, trying to keep the microphone in her hand as she flipped over the wallet.

Everyone in the room started to whisper their own theories to one another as the news report played on. A couple kids suggested that a secret underground society of ninjas stole the time capsule. Someone even started ranting about how there was *never* a capsule to begin with and it's all some kind of crazy conspiracy. I even heard someone say it was probably time traveling cavemen. I mean, come on, really? Time traveling cavemen?

"Keep the camera on me," Debbie muttered as she flipped open the white wallet.

A voice from off screen shouted. "Who's wallet is it? Who would do such a shady thing?"

Debbie paused, holding the wallet up to the camera. The shaky video struggled to focus on the student I.D. that was tucked behind a plastic cover. Finally, the face on the I.D. was as clear as day.

STUDENT I.D.
BRODY VALENTINE
EYES - BLUE
HEIGHT - 4ft 11in
WEIGHT - 92 lbs
GRADE - 6

"Brody Valentine! This wallet belongs to Brody Valentine!" Debbie shouted.

Everyone in the room gasped at the same instant as if they were trying to suck *all* the oxygen from the air. I think I was the only one who couldn't breath. I sat in my chair, completely stupefied and frozen in shock as the other kids looked at one another, puzzled and asking questions out loud.

"Who's Brody Valentine?"

"There's a kid at Buchanan with the last name 'Valentine?'"

"That name has to be a joke, right? No one here has a goofy name like that."

"Pretty sure that I.D. is fake. That sounds like a rock star's name."

Lucky for me, nobody in the class knew who I was. Or wait… was that lucky? Or just sad? Oh well, that one kid said I had a rock star's name, so I got over it pretty fast.

The television screen flickered. Another sixth grade news reporter was staring into the camera. Holding a few sheets of paper with his left hand and his finger pressed into his ear with his right hand, he spoke. "This just in for breaking news. The identity of the time capsule bandit has been made public, and Buchanan School hall monitors have issued a warrant for the arrest of sixth grader, Brody Valentine. I repeat, *Brody Valentine* is wanted for the theft of the 1999 time capsule *and* for having a weird last name!"

I gripped the sides of my desk. I had no idea what to do except sit helplessly in my seat. This all seemed to be escalating *way* too quickly.

"If you come into contact with Mr. Valentine," the news reporter said, "do *not* engage him. It's not known whether he's dangerous yet, but it's best to let the hall monitors do their job. Your cooperation is appreciated." The reporter swiveled in his chair, facing a girl wearing a fancy suit. "We have Lydia Steinburg sitting with us now to tell us what to expect, *psychologically*, from Valentine. She has no experience in psychology, but she's seen a few programs about it on television. Welcome, Lydia."

"Thank you," Lydia replied. "It's my pleasure to be here."

My school photo appeared in the corner of the screen with the word "WANTED" in red. I couldn't believe my eyes. This had to be a terrible dream!

"Lydia," the reporter said, "What do you think Valentine's next move is going to be?"

Lydia cleared her throat. "Well, if he's anything like the villains in the video games I play, then I believe *world domination* is next on his list."

"Are you kidding me?" I shouted, immediately slapping my hands over my mouth. I stared as the rest of my homeroom class turned in their chairs to face me. I was going to say something else, but was interrupted by some kids at the door.

Three hall monitors, wearing black suits and sunglasses, stood in the doorway. It was the same outfit that Colton and his monitors were wearing the week before, which meant these weren't your everyday normal monitors. They were part of the secret division of monitors, known as the "covert monitors."

"Brody Valentine?" said the largest monitor. "Come with us."

I took a deep breath and stood from my desk. I could feel the eyes of every student in my class burning holes right through my body. Grabbing my backpack off the floor, I tried to pull it over my shoulder, but the hall monitor yanked it from my hands.

"We'll take that, thank you," said the monitor.

I nodded, stepping out the door. My brain was still running in circles like a dog chasing its tail. Within minutes I had watched my wallet get dug up, a breaking news report that said my next move was world domination, and was arrested in front of an entire classroom of sixth graders.

This was *not* the greatest morning in my life.

As I walked down the hallway, I spoke. "Listen, I'm not the guy you're after."

"Save it for Principal Davis," replied the large hall monitor as he marched in front of me.

The other two monitors lagged behind, keeping their distance. One of the monitors was speaking into a walkie talkie. "We've got the package, and we're on our way. ETA five minutes."

The radio chirped, and a voice answered. "Happy holidays."

"I prefer the term, 'Merry Christmas,'" the monitor replied.

Again, the radio chirped. "All clear for package delivery."

I've never felt more confused about a conversation in my entire life.

"You're done, Valentine," the lead monitor said. "Game over."

"Seriously," I said, "I have no idea who took that time capsule, but I swear it *wasn't* me! I don't even know how my wallet got out there!"

The monitor laughed. "Right. Next thing you'll say

is that someone broke into your locker, took your wallet, and planted it in the ground where the capsule was buried. You were *framed*," he said, waving his hands in front of his body, mocking me.

"You *have* to believe me!" I pleaded. "I've been in homeroom the entire time!"

"The capsule was stolen *long* before school started, Mr. Valentine," the monitor shouted. "Unfortunately for you, you dropped your wallet and left some extremely hardcore evidence for us."

The monitors walked me down the hall, through the lobby and in front of the cafeteria. I saw the disappointed faces of children in study hall through the tinted glass windows. The students and teachers helping with the stage production stopped what they were doing to gawk at me. It made me sick to my stomach because they thought I was guilty.

So sick that I just about puked.

The lead monitor stopped and turned around. "You okay?"

I shook my head rapidly, pointing at my stomach. And then I glanced at the door to the nearby restroom that was connected to the school gymnasium. I clutched at my belly and started hobbling toward it.

"He's gonna pop!" said the monitor as he put his arm around me, keeping me from falling to the ground. "Help me get him to the bathroom!"

The other two monitors grabbed my other arm and rushed me to the door. The lead monitor pushed it wide open and allowed me to walk in.

"Puke your brains out in the toilet and get yourself cleaned up," the monitor said. "Don't try anything stupid because we'll be right out here waiting for you."

One of the other monitors spoke up. "I don't know, man. *Christmas* ain't gonna be happy if he knows we let him outta our sight."

Did that kid just say something about Christmas again?

The lead monitor tightened his lips as he pushed me into the restroom. "Then *don't* tell him."

The door shut behind me as I stumbled in. As soon as I heard it clunk, I stood up straight. My stomach *was* churning a second ago, but I knew I *wasn't* going to barf. I only faked it to buy some time in the bathroom. Those monitors would've never released me unless they were afraid of getting puked on.

Anytime I did anything crazy like that, I always wondered if I made the right decision. Could I have done something different back there? Said something else? My brain was racing with questions as I tiptoed around the room. What was I doing? Why was I even trying to escape? What if I went along with the monitors? Would that be smarter because I could simply explain that it wasn't me?

A weakness of mine is that I sometimes focus too much on what I *could've* done, you know what I mean? I waste a lot of time imagining situations play out with different endings, and at that moment I was having a hard

23

time accepting what had already happened. What would I have changed if I could do it again?

Shaking my head, I returned my attention to the situation at hand. I grunted loudly, making noises to fool the monitors even more. As I did, I scanned the room. Since this restroom was connected to the gym, there was another exit on the other side, past the lockers.

I made one last gut wrenching sound to trick the guards into thinking I was violently ill, then I sprinted across the polished cement floor until I made it to the exit on other side.

Cracking the door open, I peeked into the gymnasium. Class was already in session with several students playing basketball. Over at the side of the gym, I saw the bleachers had been pulled out from the wall, which meant the space underneath was open.

Awhile back, my dad gave me a bit of advice on how to keep people from bugging me if I'm ever in a large crowd. We were at a church picnic and all these old ladies kept coming up to me to tell me how big I've gotten. You know the ones I'm talking about – they still pinch your cheeks even though you're not two years old anymore.

Eventually, my dad saw how frustrated I was that I couldn't even cross the room without getting stopped a bunch of times so he taught me this trick – walk as if your destination is *super* important. It doesn't even matter what your destination is! For the rest of the picnic, I followed his advice, and guess what? Not one single old lady tried to pinch my face. I kept imagining there was one slice of cheesecake left that I *had* to have, which translated to *"don't bug that kid 'cause he's on a mission!"*

My dad also said if that didn't work, then just run straight at the old ladies. They'll be so confused that they won't know what to do. They'll just stand there frozen in place!

Sucking up all my fear, I stepped into the gym and briskly walked toward the bleachers. My knees shook at first as I noticed a couple kids look in my direction, but my determined pace worked. They went right back to shooting hoops. I smiled at how skilled I was at keeping invisible. If there was a ninja clan at this school, I'd totally be the first in line to join.

Finally I ducked, stepping into the open space under the bleachers. It was dark since there weren't any lights there, which worked to my advantage. I expected the area to be filthy and littered with candy wrappers and sticky soda cans, but it was surprisingly clean. When I got to around the middle of the gym, I stopped and leaned against the wall. Through the small slits in the bleachers, I could see the shadows of other kids running around and playing. No one had a clue I was even there.

I sighed, trying to wrap my head around the facts. Someone stole my wallet, but I really don't have a clue *when* they took it. The last time I remember holding it was after Linus handed me the business card with the raven. I stuck the card into the wallet and tossed it back onto the top shelf of my locker.

But that *also* meant that someone got *into* my locker somehow, which isn't terribly difficult I bet. All they would need is a key or the combination. Figuring out the combination would take too much time and skill. Stealing a skeleton key that opened *all* the lockers would make it easy, almost like using a cheat code. Whoever did it *had* to have a key.

Let's not forget about the fact that I've been framed – been made to look like the thief that took the time capsule. Was the real criminal trying to frame *me* or was I just a random choice in a school full of students. Either way – *not* cool.

And actually, the fact that my wallet was taken and dropped off at the scene of a crime wasn't the most important part. The most important part was that someone stole the time capsule. Whatever Mrs. Olsen had buried back in 1999 was valuable enough to steal. So where *was* that capsule?

Suddenly, it hit me. I was going to have to find the time capsule if I wanted to clear my name of this mess. I'd have to find the *real* thief if I didn't want to stare at the walls of detention for the rest of my life. I hadn't planned on living out another day as a secret agent, but it looked like that's what was happening.

The only thing that really bothered me was the fact that I had no idea how long my wallet had been missing. It might've been taken last week or just yesterday, and I wouldn't have had a *clue...*

"That's it!" I said softly as I paced under the bleachers. "A clue! I could get back to my locker and search for a clue that might lead me to the real thief!" I paused, fully understanding that I was talking to myself like a crazy person. "But the monitors are probably swarmed around it already..."

I clenched my jaw, trying to shake the feeling of defeat off my shoulders. I knew it was dumb to search my locker, but I really had no other choice. That was my best bet at the moment, and even though the odds were stacked against me, I stepped out from the bleachers and headed toward my locker on the other end of the school.

The hallway outside the gymnasium was quiet and empty. Everyone was settled into their first period classes so I wasn't too worried about being seen. I just had to walk quickly by open doors if I was going to remain hidden.

As I rushed through the corridor, I heard my name from one of the televisions on the wall. When I glanced at it, I saw my school photo on the screen as a reporter's voice spoke behind it.

"Sixth grader Brody Valentine is wanted for the theft of the science class time capsule. After being apprehended by local monitors, Valentine overpowered the monitors and escaped. He is on the loose somewhere within the boundaries of Buchanan School. A reward of five *hundred* dollars has been offered for any information that might lead to the capture of Valentine."

Overpowered the monitors? All I did was walk into a bathroom!

"Principal Davis had this to say," the reporter said.

The image on the screen switched to a shaky camera of the principal standing in front of a dozen microphones. "The suspect was last seen being escorted by monitors outside the cafeteria. If you see him, do *not* approach him. Find the nearest adult and inform them that Brody Valentine is nearby."

What!? Now I'm *that* kid? Find an *adult* if you see me? *Seriously?*

I groaned as I started jogging through the hallways of the school. My locker was coming up, and the sooner this whole thing was over, the *better*.

Slowing to a stop just at the end of the hall, I

peeked my head around the corner. The next corridor was empty, and my locker was only a few feet away. I waited for a second, holding my breath and staring at a single spot on the floor. If you do that in a place that's completely still, you'll notice *anything* that moves.

When I was sure that no one else was around, I ran up to my locker and spun my combination on the dial. With a click, I lifted the handle and swung open the door.

Yep. The top shelf was completely empty. The wallet they had found *was* my wallet, which at this point, wasn't surprising.

I slid my hand across the top of the shelf, but all I felt was cold smooth metal. I started moving my textbooks around at the bottom of the locker, but couldn't find anything fishy down there either. The dial of the locker was totally fine too. There were no clues anywhere to be found!

I exhaled slowly, leaning into my locker, feeling completely defeated. My wallet was gone and the school thought I was a criminal. It was my word against the evidence. Out of frustration, I banged my head into the shelf where my wallet was supposed to be.

And then a second later I heard a clunk, as if a sheet of metal had fallen. When I looked up, I saw that the back wall of the top shelf was tilted, but only slightly. If I hadn't heard the sound, I wouldn't even have noticed something was off.

Reaching my hand in, I pushed against the spot behind the shelf. The instant my fingers touched the metal, the sheet slipped and fell back, revealing a *hole* in the wall!

I peered in, but couldn't see anything on the other side. The area was dark, but there was definitely a room back there.

Finally, I was getting somewhere!

I looked down both sides of the hall to see if there was a way to get into the room. Down the way and to my left, I saw a wooden door that was shut. The sign on front said it was a maintenance room.

I didn't waste any time. I walked to the door so fast that I completely forgot to shut my locker. No big deal, I thought. I'll just reach through the hole and shut it from the inside.

After opening the door, I slipped inside. It was dark and cold, and felt like the air was wet. It was noisy too. Along the walls were rusted pipes that probably moved water around the school. Some tools sat upon a wooden desk that was built into the side of the room. The walls weren't anything fancy – just exposed cinder blocks with bumpy cement that held them together. Before I took another step, I let the entrance shut behind me and made sure to lock it just in case.

And then I saw the hole in the wall. It was a few feet away and right at my eye level. I ran my fingers against the cinder blocks as I scanned the area below it for any trace of who might've taken my wallet.

I was surprised by the lack of cinder block dust below the hole. It almost seemed as though the opening had been carved long ago.

I took a peek through the small hole carved into the wall and then remembered that my locker door was still open. Without thinking, I reached my arm through the opening to grab the metal door.

At that instant, I felt two hands wrap around my forearm on the other side of my locker. My heart just about exploded in my chest as I tried to jerk my arm out, but whoever was on the other side had too good of a grip on me!

Propping my foot against the cinder blocks, I grabbed my caught arm with my free hand and tried prying myself away from the wall. It was like the locker had come to life and was trying to eat me!

"Let go!" I screamed.

A muffled voice shouted through the brick wall. "He's on the other side! Valentine is on the other side of this locker! Find a way through and arrest him!"

The voices I heard were of the hall monitors. Of course they were, right? Isn't that just my luck? Remember when I wondered if there was anything I'd change if I could do certain situations over again? Well, in this case, I *wouldn't* have blindly stuck my arm through a hole in the wall.

"I didn't take the time capsule!" I shouted, still trying to regain control of my arm.

The monitor's grip on my wrist tightened and twisted like he was trying to give me a snakebite. "You've got nowhere to run, Valentine! Give yourself up and we'll go easy on ya!"

My face was getting hot as I struggled to free myself. The concrete edges of the hole was scraping against my arm. It *killed*. The door to the maintenance room pounded. The monitors were trying to break their way in.

I heard more muffled voices behind the wall. "It's locked! Who's got a key?"

"I forgot the key back at the pool!" answered another monitor.

Back at the pool? Were these guys kickin' back and relaxin' while catchin' some rays before they came after me? Strange, I thought. Even *stranger* because I'm pretty sure Buchanan *doesn't* have a pool.

"Then kick it down!" shouted the monitor with my arm.

Kick it down? Were they really going to try and— *BOOM!*

Yep, they were gonna kick the door down. My time was running short, and I was starting to freak out. Taking a deep breath, I held it in my lungs and kicked at the cement wall with all my strength. The force of my push finally freed my arm from the monitor, and I went flying into the wooden worktable behind me. Stumbling, I waved my arms out, regaining my balance.

The monitors kicked at the door again.

BOOM!

It was only a matter of minutes before they broke their way in. Spinning in a circle, I scanned the dark room, hoping for another exit, but I couldn't find one. The area was just a cold and dark prison cell that I had walked into willingly.

Dumb, Brody. Really dumb.

BOOM!

I ran to the door and pressed my body against it, like *that* was going to do anything. "I didn't take the capsule! You gotta believe me!"

"Sure ya didn't, Valentine!" shouted one of the monitors behind the door before they kicked it again. "Just turn yourself in and you can tell us the *whole* story!"

"Let me talk to Colton!" I pleaded. Colton was the leader of the covert monitors I had to deal with the week before. He was a tough kid, but I knew that he'd at least hear me out.

"Colton ain't on the force anymore!" replied the voice. "Turned in his badge and sash last week after the whole ordeal with President Sebastian!"

I grit my teeth, frustrated and more hopeless than ever. And just when I was about to give up, I heard a soft thump sound come from behind me, *inside* the room.

I turned to see what it was, but it was too late. The

34

monitors kicking at the door finally managed to break it open. The force of the blow knocked me across the room. As I staggered, I braced for impact, expecting the cold hard floor to slap me in the face, but it never did. Instead, I felt two arms catch me at the last second. I looked up fully knowing that it was a monitor that caught me, but I was wrong.

It was Maddie.

"Sup?" she said, smirking.

I would've responded, but a loud pop interrupted me. Instantly the room filled with a thick smoke cloud that made it impossible to see. It smelled like chalk dust.

"Climb," Maddie's voice whispered as she put a rope into my hands.

I couldn't see a thing, but I started climbing the rope that she gave me. A few feet off the ground, I felt another hand wrap around my own, and then it pulled me up into the space above the maintenance room. With less chalk dust up there, I could see that it was Linus that had helped me up.

He put his finger to his lips, telling me to keep quiet as he helped Maddie through the opening. Then he replaced the ceiling tile and gave me the most disapproving look I'd ever seen on *anyone's* face. It was even worse than the face my mom made when I told her I got an F on my math test.

We started crawling through the open space in the ceiling, which wasn't what I expected it to be. The walls were smooth and looked as though we were actually in a secret passage. Whatever this was, it was meant to be used as an escape tunnel.

I heard the muffled voices of the monitors again. "Where'd he go? You! Did you see him run out the door?"

"No, sir!" replied a boy's voice. "But I wasn't by the door when the smoke screen went off."

"Was *anyone* by the door? Did you guys just let him get away *again?*"

Nobody answered.

"*You're* the one that's gonna have to answer to *Christmas* then," the lead monitor said before I heard the door slam shut.

There it was again – *Christmas.*

"What's your *problem?*" Linus asked promptly.

I was confused. "What are you *talking* about?"

"Going to your locker like that was such a *noob* thing to do!" Linus said, shaking his head. "I thought you were smarter than that."

"Go easy," Maddie said. "He hasn't had the kind of training we've had. I think it was actually *smart* for him to check it out. You weren't down there just a second ago. I saw a hole in the wall right behind his locker."

Linus paused, still angry. "Really?"

"Really," Maddie repeated.

Linus continued crawling along the escape passage. "Fine," he said. "Follow us."

We crawled for another twenty feet or so before coming to an opening. A ladder was connected to the open spot on the ceiling so it was easier to climb down. The room we were in looked like one of the unused detention rooms that doubled as a storage space. Cardboard boxes lined the walls of the small room. The only open spot was the entrance to the hallway.

I rubbed my arm where the concrete had scraped against me. Wincing in pain, I took a seat at the long table in the middle of the room. Maddie sat on the other side and stared at me. Linus dropped a manila folder on the surface of the table and cracked his knuckles.

"Was it you?" Maddie asked right away.

"No!" I said, understanding what her question was referring to. "I didn't take that time capsule!"

Maddie folded her hands and leaned forward.

"Sorry. Had to ask."

Linus set his arms on top of the manila folder. "What do you know about this morning? Has anyone tried to contact you before any of this?"

"What?" I asked, confused. "No. Nobody contacted me about anything, and all I know of this morning was that they found my wallet at the dig site on *live* television."

"Did you put it there?" Linus asked flatly.

I shook my head. "You *think* I put it there?"

"So it was stolen," Linus continued. "When did you first notice it was missing?"

I exhaled slowly, rolling my eyes. "I don't know. I only saw that it was gone when I was looking for clues at my locker. I had no idea it was even taken!"

Linus nodded, staring me in the eye. "But your wallet was *in* your locker when it was stolen?"

Maddie interrupted. "Yeah, the hole in the wall can

tell you *that* much."

I was getting flustered. Throwing my arms out wide, I spoke. "*What* is going on here? *Why* was I framed for the time capsule theft?"

Linus glanced at Maddie, who nodded at him in return. It was a silent gesture of agreement.

Linus flipped open the manila folder and pushed the whole thing to my side of the table. There were three photos on top of a short stack of papers. One photo was of a girl with black hair. The other two were of the same boy. Strange that he would have *two* class photos.

"Recognize either of them?" Linus asked.

I tapped at the picture of the girl. "Her name is Sophia," I said. "I had a huge crush on her in third grade, but we never went out or anything."

"Right," Maddie said. "We believe *she's* the one who took the time capsule and planted your wallet."

"But *why* would she do that?" I asked. "I've never done anything to her! I mean, I probably acted like a dork and flirted or something, but is that really enough reason to *frame* a guy?"

"You'd be surprised," Maddie snipped. I wasn't sure if it was a joke or not.

Linus shook his head. "We believe Sophia is working with this kid. She's been known to pull heists for him in the past." He paused and looked at the class photos again. "Do you recognize *him*?"

I tapped at the table, studying the picture of the boy. "I don't know *who* he is, but I've seen him walking the hallways between classes. Kind of a big kid if I remember correctly. He has to be *new* at Buchanan, right? Because I've never had him in a class before, and I've gone here since kindergarten."

Linus tightened his lips. "His name is Christopher Moss, and he's what's known as a *super* sixth grader. Are you familiar with the term?"

I leaned back, floored by what Linus had said. "No way..."

"Yep," Maddie said. "He's in the process of *repeating* the sixth grade. He failed last year because he got all F's on his report card."

"A second year sixth grader," I said softly, staring at his photos. "That's why he's got *two* class photos. A *super* sixth grader. How sad."

"It's not sad," Linus said. "He did it to himself."

"Have a *heart*," Maddie groaned.

Linus continued. "Colton quit his position last week—"

"I heard," I said, trying to sound like I had my own sources for information even though I only knew because a monitor had just shouted it at me.

"And over the weekend, Christopher was somehow *given* Colton's old position," Linus said. "He's in charge of the secret service monitors now."

I flicked at one of the photos of Christopher. "But what's he got to do with me?"

Linus slid Christopher's photo aside and pointed at the sheets of paper underneath them. "Christopher *used* to be one of us. Last year he was the top agent in the agency we're a part of—"

"Which is called…" I interrupted, folding my arms and leaning back.

Linus looked up from his notes and glared at me.

I laughed. "You can keep it a secret all you like, but the fact that we're sitting here in this room, and you're telling me about all this means that I already have *some* knowledge about you and the agency you work for."

Maddie set her hand on his shoulder. "He's right," she said. "There's no reason to keep *everything* from him. Besides, *you* were the one who involved him last time."

Linus shut his eyes and exhaled through his nose. "Glitch," he said.

"Glitch?" I repeated.

"Glitch," Linus said again. "That's the name of the secret agency we work for."

I unfolded my arms and gestured for Linus to continued.

"Anyway," Linus said, returning his attention to the manila folder. "Christopher Moss used to be a part of Glitch last year, and was even the top agent in the field, but when he failed sixth grade, he got booted from the agency. It wasn't anything personal – the agency just frowns upon keeping super sixth graders as agents."

"Were the two of you agents last year?" I asked.

Maddie answered. "No. Glitch is only for sixth graders. We didn't know it even existed last year."

"We've been ordered to keep an eye on him this year though," Linus said. "Super sixth graders have been known to go bonkers from time to time, and it looks like Christopher just took some crazy pills. He's been busy creating an agency of his own here at Buchanan."

This all sounded so crazy, but I gotta admit, I was hooked. "Does his club have a name?" I asked.

"Suckerpunch," Maddie said.

"So he controls the covert monitors," I said, "*and* his own secret organization? This kid sounds dangerous."

Linus nodded. "He *is*."

I stared at the photos of Christopher that were on the table in front of me. He didn't look like an evil villain. He was clean cut, blond haired and blue eyed, and looked like he should've been the cool quarter back that everyone wanted to be friends with. Sure, he looked *slightly* older than a sixth grader, but not like a creepy teenager. As I studied the photos, a little light bulb clicked in my head, and I laughed.

"What's so funny?" Linus asked, annoyed.

"Christopher Moss," I said, smirking. "*Chris* Moss. *Christmas.*"

Linus and Maddie looked at one another. Linus twirled his finger around his ear to signal that maybe I was crazy.

"Those monitors were talking about someone they called 'Christmas,'" I explained. "Whoever they're working for goes by that weird name. It makes sense that Chris would go by *Christmas.*"

Linus leaned back in his chair, giving me the evil eye.

Maddie nudged him with her elbow. "Y'see? There's hope for Valentine yet."

Pushing his chair away from the table, Linus snatched up the manila folder and started walking to the door. He spoke as if I wasn't even in the room. "Valentine hasn't chosen a side yet, Maddie! He could be working for Suckerpunch right now, and we wouldn't have a clue! He could be playing *us!*"

I sat up, defending myself. "I'm not playing you!"

"Then why haven't you joined Glitch yet?" Linus asked coldly.

I paused, swallowing my pride. "Because that life isn't for me," I said honestly. "Sure, last week was fun and all, but this is serious stuff! I was *framed* today, and now the whole school is searching for me! When I got home from school after busting Sebastian, I was *happy* to go back to being a nobody!"

"That's *bogus*," Linus sneered. "Nobody's *that* much of a wuss!"

"No, I'm serious!" I said, throwing my arms out. "*I'm* that much of a wuss! I don't *want* to be the kid who chases after bad guys and gets caught up in risky situations!" Even as I said it, I knew it wasn't completely true.

"Then I can't and *won't* help you 'cause you haven't chosen a side yet," Linus said. "You think can float somewhere in the middle?"

"Isn't that what everyone else is doing?" I asked, irritated. "Aren't we all just staying off radars and out of everyone's lives? This isn't a movie! There isn't a *good* team or a *bad* team."

"Isn't there?" Linus whispered, glancing at the door. I knew he was referring to the students of Buchanan School. "*You* have the ability to be different from them! We *all* do! But it doesn't happen until we decide it does. You have to *choose* to be the kid that does the *right* thing or the one that does *nothing*. And if you choose to do the *right* thing, then you'd better stick to that decision and *do it* no matter what. Even when nobody else is doing it - no, *especially* when nobody else is doing it."

For the first time in my life, I actually felt speechless. I wanted to keep arguing because Linus was getting on my nerves, but deep down I knew he was a hundred percent correct.

Linus walked to the door, opened it a crack, and stopped. Without turning back, he said, "There's just no way of knowing without a doubt whether you're *with* or *against* us. C'mon, Maddie. We've got a school to save."

Maddie didn't move from her chair. "I think I'll stay," she said. "Brody could use a friend right now."

It was cheesy and a little embarrassing for her to say that, but it *did* make me feel better.

Linus shook his head, disappointed. With the pull of his arm, he yanked the door open and disappeared into the hallway.

"Sorry about him," Maddie said, rocking back and forth in her chair. "Sometimes the stress gets to him, y'know?"

"I can imagine," I said.

She looked me in the eye. "But he's right. Until you're working with Glitch, I shouldn't give you any help at all," she said, and then tightened a smile. "But I'm gonna give it to you anyway. *Don't* make this become one of the worst decisions I've ever made."

"That's what high school's for, right?" I laughed, trying to lighten the mood, but Maddie didn't seem to appreciate the joke.

"This is funny to you?" Maddie asked.

I coughed, containing my laughter. "No, sorry."

The bell started ringing in the hallway, which meant first period was over. Through the door, I heard the sound of hundreds of footsteps making their way to second period.

"So what do we do now?" I asked, standing from the table. "Go after Christmas?"

Maddie shook her head. "Christmas is harder to find than a monkey in the ocean."

I wasn't sure what she meant by that, but I went with it. "I know, right? Ocean monkeys are the *worst.*"

"Right now, we only *think* Christmas is behind all this," Maddie said. "There's no hard evidence so we have to find the capsule first."

"Sophia then?" I suggested.

"Sophia," Maddie repeated, scratching at her eyebrow. "If we can find her, maybe she can give us some answers."

"So what class does she have?" I asked.

"Orchestra," Maddie groaned, annoyed. "*Hipsters.*"

In case you don't know, hipsters are kind of the new thing at my school. They're kids who are *too cool* to be cool. They spend half their lives doing the exact opposite of what everyone else is doing *just because* everyone else is doing it, and they try harder than anyone to make it look like they're not trying at all. They'll spend forever choosing their outfit so it looks like they just threw on a bunch of nerdy styled clothing. And then after all that, they throw it back in your face by talking down to you as if they're elite because of it! They're like bullies, but without the muscles!

The noise in the hallway slowly disappeared until there were only a few pitter-patters left. The bell rang again, which signaled the start of second period.

"C'mon," Maddie said unenthusiastically. "Better get going."

If Sophia had orchestra, then she'd still be in class. Students that had orchestra had it for the first two periods of the day. But any class that had anything to do with music was also in the lower levels of Buchanan.

"Wonderful," I sighed. "Let's go down to the dungeon."

Several minutes later, Maddie and I set foot back into the dungeon of Buchanan School. It felt weird because the two of us were doing the same thing just the week before.

Naturally, I made a lame comment about it. "So we're going to the same place for our second date, huh? Has the fire burnt out between us already?"

Maddie glanced back at me with an eyebrow cocked. I couldn't tell if she was annoyed or amused.

"Y'know," I said, stumbling over my words. "Because if we were on a second date and returning to a lame place then that'd mean we're a pretty boring couple and um… I uh…"

"I get it," Maddie said coldly as she continued down the hallway.

"Awkwaaaaaaard," I whispered, hopping a few

steps to catch up.

The dungeon was exactly in the same condition as it was the first time we were down there. The lack of sunlight made it so that fluorescent bulbs were the only source of light. There was a bluish green tint to everything, probably because the paint on the walls was moldy and chipping away. The wet concrete underneath the paint peeked out at us as if was begging to be seen.

The corridors were still filled with sugar addicts. President Sebastian's plot to sell sweets in the dungeon had been foiled, but it was going to be a few weeks before the problem was completely fixed. Principal Davis said all of Sebastian's candy had been confiscated, but that didn't mean it was totally gone. There were still students that had some leftover in their lockers and backpacks.

A bunch of shady kids had already tried bringing their own candy from home to sell since there was clearly a market for it, but teachers were quick to bust them at the first sign of it.

Still though... the few sugar addicts that remained in the dungeon scared the snot outta my nose.

"Where's the orchestra room?" I asked, rubbing my arms like I was cold, which was weird because the dungeon *wasn't* cold.

"Up ahead," Maddie replied. She looked back at me and snickered. "Someone afraid of the scary dungeon of Buchanan?"

My teeth started chattering, but I shook my head to

stop them. "They don't call it the *dungeon* for nothing!"

At that instant, a filthy hand waved in front of my face, nearly smacking my cheek. I cried out like a baby and hobbled backward, banging against the metal lockers on the wall.

"You guys lookin' to buy?" the owner of the filthy hand asked. His grin displayed a few missing teeth among some other rotten ones. In his other hand was an open canvas bag filled with chocolate bars. It looked like he had just finished trick or treating. "Got enough candy to last ya for a day! Whatcha want? Sugar-bombs? Choco-lattes? Sugar-shocks? I got it all!"

Maddie pushed the boy aside. "Stay outta our way, sugar head."

Kids had started using the term "sugar head" when referring to the sugar addicts in Buchanan's dungeon.

The boy with the candy licked his lips and frowned. "You'll be back," he sneered. "Ain't nobody comes down to the dungeon without pickin' up a few snacks before leaving."

As she walked past the boy, Maddie rolled her eyes and held her open palm in front of his face. She didn't say anything else.

The sugar head looked at me. "How about you? You don't seem to have a chip on your shoulder."

I leaned over and checked out his stash of goods. I saw all kinds of suckers and hard candy along with individually wrapped chewy candy that had a sugar coating. I'm not a "candy" kind of kid – I'm more into chocolate bars, which was also lining the bottom of his bag. King sized chocolate bars and peanut butter cups were everywhere. I started reaching my hand out...

"Brody!" Maddie shouted from ahead.

Instantly I stood at attention and put my hands behind my head. Whenever I'm caught doing something I shouldn't be, my first reaction is to nervously laugh. "Hey, uh... I... ha ha ha!"

"Quit wasting time!" Maddie ordered.

I don't know why, but I looked at the sugar head and apologized.

Maddie and I walked down a few more dark hallways until we were outside the entrance to the orchestra room. You'd think the hallway would be filled with beautiful music coming from cellos and violins and stuff, but it wasn't. Instead, all it sounded like was a bunch of kids talking to one another.

Maddie touched my elbow and spoke. "Listen," she said. "While we're in here, just let me do the talking. These are *hipsters* we're dealing with. There's a very specific way of dealing with them so they'll cooperate, okay?"

I nodded.

"Seriously," she said. "Don't say a word! There's no 'good cop, bad cop' routine happening here. It's just *me* that's gonna talk."

Holding my hands up in surrender, I said, "Okay, I get it! I won't say a thing!"

Maddie turned around, took a deep breath, and stepped to the door of the orchestra room. I felt a chill run down my spine as I followed behind her. I wasn't sure what to expect, but Maddie's little warning had my knees trembling. Orchestra kids couldn't be *that* bad, could they?

The second we entered the room, it was like we stepped into another world. Kids were sprawled out on the floor listening to music on their headphones while others sat in chairs along the wall. Some of them mumbled about how "yesterday" my vest was. Only a couple of students had their instruments out, but they weren't playing them the way they were supposed to, probably as an act of rebellion to orchestras around the world.

Oh, and *everyone* wore thick black rimmed glasses *without* the actual glass part in the frames.

51

"Some kids wear glasses because they *need* glasses," I whispered to Maddie as she slowly walked to the center of the room.

She lifted her hand, gesturing for me to keep quiet, but she didn't scold me. "I know. Hipsters try too hard to make it *look* like they're *not* trying at all. Did you notice that nobody has their headphones plugged into anything?"

I laughed, realizing Maddie was right. All I could do was shake my head as I started scanning the room for the orchestra teacher. Why wasn't he out there? Where could he even be? And then I saw that he was in his office, reclined in a chair with his feet up on his desk. He was wearing a checkered shirt with a scarf so tiny that it was pointless. His mustache looked like something from a western movie and on his head was a brown knit cap. I almost made the mistake of thinking he was wearing jeans, but then I saw that they were sweatpants with a denim print. How awful. No wonder these kids were allowed to do nothing. Their teacher was a hipster too!

"Looks like you're in the wrong classroom," said one of the hipster girls, reclining in a seat. Her voice was chill as if she didn't care. Of course she didn't. She was a hipster.

Maddie stopped directly at the center of the room. She set her hands on her hips and spoke. "We're looking for a girl named Sophia."

The hipster girl made a smack sound with her lips as she raised her eyebrows. "Sophia is such a lame-wad name," she sighed. "It's so yesterday."

The hipsters around her nodded and mumbled in agreement.

Maddie paused as her face grew red with anger. "There's a girl named Sophia somewhere in this class. I don't care about the weirdo hippy names you've given yourselves because your *real* names are all that matter. Now tell me where we can find *Sophia*."

Another boy sat forward in his chair and wagged his finger at me. "You're the kid that stole the time capsule, aren't you?"

I started to answer, but he interrupted me.

"Way to go, man," he said, smiling. "Everyone was too into the capsule anyway, right? Time capsules are so *yesterday*."

"Right?" the hipster girl groaned.

Maddie took a step forward. "Of course time capsules are yesterday! That's the point of them!"

Everyone in the room casually glanced at each other. I heard several of the students whisper the phrase, "*Played out.*"

Abruptly, Maddie snapped, pointing at the girl in the chair. "Tell us where Sophia is or else!"

The hipster girl blinked slowly. It looked like she was falling asleep. Tipping her chair back, she finally spoke. "Your clothes are so *yesterday*," she whispered.

Maddie stormed forward and swept her foot under the girl's chair.

"Aaaah!" the hipster girl screamed as she fell backward.

Faster than lightning, Maddie caught the hipster by her shirt and pulled her back to safety. The metal legs on the chair clamped down on the hard floor.

"You see my partner over here?" Maddie hissed, pointing her thumb at me. "He's *crazy*. He *eats* hipsters for breakfast so if you don't tell me where I can find Sophia, then I promise that your future children will *weep* when you tell them stories of what happened after I leave him alone with you guys in this room!"

I stood there with my eyes wide open, stunned by what Maddie was threatening. Obviously it was a bluff, but I hoped the hipsters couldn't see it. I did my best to look menacing by furrowing my eyebrows and chomping my teeth together. I was trying to imitate a rabid dog, but probably looked more like I had something stuck in my cheek.

The hipster girl bought my act. She sat up straight and ran her fingers through her frazzled hair. "Ugh," she grunted. She nodded her head to point at a spot across the room. "Sophia's over there."

In that instant, one of the students jumped up from the floor and sprinted toward the exit. She moved so quickly that she was a blur, but I knew it had to be Sophia. Why else would anyone freak out like that? Kicking her foot out, Sophia knocked the door wide open and dove into the dark hallway.

Maddie took the lead, taking off like a dog after a bunny. As she jumped through the door, she held her wrist next to her mouth and spoke into the watch that was strapped on it. I couldn't hear her, but if it was the same watch she wore the week before, then I knew it had a built-in communicator.

Without hesitating, I ran through the orchestra room, following Maddie into the hallway. I paused outside the door to see which direction she had taken off in, and when I saw her shadowy figure to my right I immediately returned to the chase.

Sophia was already halfway down the hall, running as fast as she could. Maddie kept after the hipster, but stumbled over a small stack of boxes. Rolling across the floor, I heard her grunt as she slid against the wall. I almost stopped to help, but I didn't want to lose Sophia so I jumped over the boxes and continued.

The squawks from my sneakers bounced against the lockers as I kept my eyes on Sophia. She was running deeper into the dungeon, and not toward the stairs like I thought she would. Common sense said that she'd try to escape to the upper levels of Buchanan, but that wasn't where she was headed.

My side was starting to cramp, but I pushed harder because if she got away, then my name would *never* be cleared. Surprisingly I was catching up to her. At that point, I was only about ten feet away.

Just then, Sophia ran past a random sugar head, grabbing his sack of sweets.

"Hey!" the kid cried. "That's mine!"

As I ran past the same boy, I saw Sophia make it to where the hall turned the corner. She kicked her foot against the hall and instantly shot herself into the opposite direction. While she was still in the air, she tossed the sack of candy at my face.

I responded the way I did in gym when someone throws a ball at me. I flinched, raising my hands to my face and then dropped to the floor. I was moving so fast that my body slid against the polished tiles until I bumped into the lockers.

"Nice," said Maddie as she slowed to a stop beside me. Grabbing my hand, she helped me off the floor.

I remained silent, feeling pretty embarrassed. Dusting off my jeans, I wiped the bit of spit off my lip and stayed close to Maddie's side.

Maddie took the lead again, but this time she didn't run. Catching her breath, she stepped around the corner carefully just in case Sophia was waiting there with a surprise attack.

The fluorescent bulbs flickered and buzzed as we walked under them into the next hallway. I was expecting a long, dark, and scary corridor that we were going to have to explore, but to my surprise, the hall ended almost immediately after we turned the corner. There was about fifteen feet of hallway that was surrounding by lockers. Against the back wall was another set of lockers. There was no sign of Sophia.

Maddie pointed at one of the tiles on the ceiling. It was cracked and moved out of place. "There," she said through heavy breaths. "She must've climbed up to get away."

"Then let's follow her!" I said, jumping as high as I could while reaching my arms out. Even at my highest, my hand only reached about eight feet up. The ceiling was a good twelve or thirteen feet high.

Maddie leaned against one of the lockers against the back wall, still trying to catch her breath. She rubbed the spots on her knees where she had fallen. "Unless you got some rope or something I don't know about, she's as good as gone."

I clenched my jaw, frustrated and angry that Sophia had gotten away. Grunting, I started pacing around the small area. "So what now? She's just *gone* and I'm dead meat? How about we try to figure out where she's gonna jump out from?"

"It could be anywhere," Maddie said softly. "She could be on the other side of the school already."

"You can't just give up like this!"

"Stop yelling at me!" Maddie shouted. "Man! Just give me a second to think! Which one of us is the secret agent again?"

I pinched the bridge of my nose. I could feel a headache coming on from shouting so much. "I'm sorry," I said. "I just thought we had her for sure, and now I'm back to square one."

Maddie shook her head, but kept quiet.

Folding my arms, I started rubbing them up and down again like I was cold. Don't ask me why, I just was. Staring at the open ceiling tile, I tried to imagine how Sophia had gotten herself up there. It was possible this was always an available escape spot for her, and a rope was always waiting for the day she'd need it. Walking over to Maddie, I stood for a moment, and then leaned against the locker next to her.

CLICK!

"No!" shouted a girl's voice from inside the locker.

I about jumped out of my skin as I stumbled away from the locker until I realized the voice was Sophia's.

"Ha!" Maddie said, pointing at the metal locker door. "You tried to fool us into thinking you got away through the broken ceiling tile!"

Sophia started pounding at the door. "You nimrod!" she cried. "You leaned against my locker and shut it! Now I'm stuck in here! Let me out! Let me out *now!*"

Maddie kicked the locker once, but hard enough that the clang echoed through the halls. "Not until you tell us what we want to know!"

"Never!" Sophia screamed. "I don't have to tell you a thing! Now let me outta here!"

"Then *we're* outta here," Maddie said as she started walking away. Her footsteps slapped against the cold floor loudly.

I stood still, unsure of whether Maddie was going to actually leave or not. It was the most intense five seconds of my life. It seemed a little harsh of Maddie to just leave Sophia stuck in a locker like that – almost bully-ish, but then again, Sophia *did* frame me for the theft of the time capsule. Two wrongs didn't make a right, did they? No, there was no way Maddie was going to leave. She *had* to be bluffing, right?

Finally, Sophia hit the locker door again and shouted. "Wait! I'll tell you everything! Whatever you want! Just don't leave me in here! It's dark!"

Maddie turned around, smiling at me. "That's more like it."

I swallowed hard. I could feel my muscles relax as Maddie walked back to the locker. I decided the best thing to do was to say nothing, while trying to soak the information in.

"Let's start with the time capsule," Maddie said. "Did you take it?"

Sophia paused. I could tell she didn't want to confess, but finally, she spoke. "Yeah," she said softly. "I took it."

"Why?" Maddie asked.

"Because I was told to."

"And you just do anything you're told to do?"

Sophia chuckled through the locker. "When it involves a huge payday, then yeah."

"So you were *paid* to take the capsule? By who?"

"Yeah right, like I'm gonna tell you that."

"We already know it was Christopher Moss," Maddie said, shooting me a look. The truth was that we *didn't* know it was Christopher, but hopefully Sophia wouldn't be able to tell.

It worked. I heard Sophia sigh as the locker bumped once, probably from her resting her head against the inside.

"Yup," Sophia said. "Christmas left me an envelope of cash with some instructions in my locker... *this* locker."

"How much?" I asked, curious.

"Hundred bucks," Sophia replied.

"*Hundred bucks?*" I cried. "How's this kid got that much money?"

"I don't know!" Sophia shouted so loudly that the metal locker trembled.

Maddie scratched at her chin. "What's Christopher want with the capsule? What's inside?"

"I don't know that either," Sophia said. "All the instructions told me to do was to take Brody's wallet, dig up the capsule, bury the wallet into the hole, and then drop the capsule off in the garbage can next to the science labs on the second floor."

61

"*When* did you take my wallet?" I asked.

"This morning," Sophia replied. "The note said there was a hole in the wall in the maintenance room, and that on the other side of the hole was the wallet I was supposed to take."

The fact that my wallet had only been missing since earlier that morning made me feel better, but the idea that the hole in the wall was *already* there didn't.

Clapping her hands together, Maddie spoke cheerfully as she walked away from the locker. "Onward to the second floor then!"

Walking briskly, I caught up to her before she turned the corner. "What about Sophia? We can't just leave her in—"

"Agent Madison?" came a gruff voice from down the opposite end of the hall.

"Down here, agent Donavan," Maddie said.

A boy dressed in normal street clothes stepped around the corner. Another girl that had the same style clothing accompanied him. When they saw me, they both flinched.

"He's innocent," Maddie said.

The two agents immediately relaxed.

"Sophia's stuck in her locker," Maddie continued. "She wants out bad so she'll give you the combination. Take her directly to the principal's office. She confessed to stealing the capsule."

"Great," Donavan said. "Where is it?"

"We're on our way to retrieve it right now," Maddie

said. "I'll keep the agency in the loop as soon as we find it."

Donavan and the girl nodded, and then walked past us to help Sophia out of her locker.

Maddie walked to a closed door in the hall and opened it. She waved her hand at me to step through first. I watched as the two agents opened Sophia's locker. Sophia stepped out, drenched in sweat. She slowly lifted her chin until she made eye contact with me. Her eyes were cold, and felt as if they pierced my soul. They were hypnotizing.

"C'mon," Maddie said.

I clenched my eyes shut and shook my head, trying to get the image of Sophia out of my thoughts. This whole thing had me more frazzled than I realized. Finally, I stepped through the door that Maddie held open.

Inside the dark room, I heard the bell ring again, signaling the end of second period. It was amazing how fast time flew by when we were chasing after criminals.

Maddie approached a television that was mounted on the wall and switched it on. My class photo was on the screen. I was still a wanted criminal in the school.

In the dark room, Maddie took a seat. "We'll wait here until third period starts. Everyone's still looking for you so it wouldn't be the smartest thing to walk the hallways now. I mean, unless you *want* to go detention."

I sat in the desk next to her, but remained silent. I was breathing heavy from the chase we just had and still felt a little embarrassed by it.

"So…" Maddie said, trying to make conversation. "Why *haven't* you tried to find Glitch yet?"

I shrugged my shoulders. "I already told you. I don't think I'm cut out for it."

Maddie laughed. "Are you kidding? You've already escaped from hall monitors, chased after a thief, and helped find the location of the missing time capsule, and it's not even *noon* yet."

"I don't know," I said, uneasy.

"Remember what I said to you last week?" Maddie asked.

"Fake it till you make it…" I said.

"No," Maddie said, angered. "You *are* what you *think* you are. You were successful in busting Sebastian last week because you knew who you wanted to be, but it sounds like you let that dark shadow in again, didn't you? The one that tells you to stay quiet and out of trouble because life is easier that way, right? It's easier to be invisible, isn't it?"

Weird how she even used the word "invisible."

"I wish you *did* try to find Glitch," Maddie said. "It would've made *this* situation a heck of a lot easier."

I shook my head. "Doesn't matter. That raven card was in my wallet anyway, and my wallet is locked up in evidence somewhere."

Maddie smirked suspiciously. "There wasn't much on it. I bet you've got it memorized."

I stared at the floor. She was right. I *did* have it

memorized, but I wasn't about to give her the satisfaction of knowing me so well just yet.

The bell outside the door started ringing out. Third period had officially started. Maddie peeled the door open. Together, we made our way out of the dungeon and headed to the second floor of Buchanan.

About ten minutes later, we made it to the second floor, where most of the science and math classes were held. Science needed a few extra rooms because of the lab work that was needed. Toward the center of the second floor, there was an open courtyard filled with hundreds of different plants for the botany portion of class.

The garbage can Sophia had talked about was just at the end of the corridor and was easy to find. It was built into a container in the wall so it was less of an eyesore. Plastered all over the brick walls were wanted posters with my face on them.

"How do they do that so fast?" I asked.

"It's likely that Christopher is behind it," Maddie replied. "This all happened so quickly that it makes me doubt the principal had anything to do with it. Of course a bunch of wanted posters sprouting up would be considered a good thing so nobody really asks *where* they came from. I bet Christopher had the posters printed up *before* today."

"Who *is* this kid?" I whispered. "How does he have this much pull?"

"Good question," Maddie said. "I have a feeling he's gonna be a real problem for Glitch in the future."

As we approached the garbage can, Maddie glanced over her shoulder to see if we were being followed. When she was sure that we were alone, she went ahead and pulled the container out of the wall. Ripping the plastic bag from the metal, she stared into the empty bin and chewed her lip.

The time capsule *wasn't* there.

"Of course," I groaned.

Maddie pushed the container back into the wall, and then pointed to a spot over my head. "Don't worry," she laughed. "Looks like we might have a little good luck coming our way."

I turned around to see what she was pointing at. On the wall, over our heads, was a tiny camera with a little blinking red light on the front of it.

"Um," I said, "Is that something *we* have to worry about right now?"

Maddie shrugged her shoulders and grabbed my hand to follow her. "No, because Sophia already confessed. If Principal Davis reviews the footage, he'll know we were just looking in the spot she said it'd be. This is proof that you're helping."

"Okay then," I said, relieved. "Where can we watch the footage? I bet we'll see Christopher taking the capsule from the garbage, right?"

"Hopefully," Maddie said as she walked swiftly down the hall.

She pulled me along until we got to another closed door that had a keypad on the outside of it. After punching in a set of numbers, the pad blinked red and green, and I heard it unlock. Pushing the door open, Maddie stepped through first.

Inside the new room, I saw dozens of small television screens blink with black and white videos of random spots around the school. Apparently there were cameras mounted everywhere in Buchanan.

Maddie sat at the empty swivel chair in front of what looked like the command center for a spaceship.

"Is this the Glitch headquarters?" I asked, walking around the tiny room. There was barely any space for two people so if it *was* the headquarters, it was a little disappointing.

"Of course not," Maddie said as she jabbed her fingers at the keyboard in front of her. "This is just the hub for the surveillance cameras."

"Cool," I said, setting my hands on the back of Maddie's chair and leaning into it.

"Computer," Maddie said flatly. "Show me the video for the science lab hallway starting at 7:45 AM this morning."

No way! A voice controlled computer system? Was Glitch *actually* a legit secret agency in the school?

The televisions all blinked once. Then they showed the video feed from the morning across all of the screens at the same time creating one giant image in front of us.

Maddie folded her hands and rested her chin on

them. As she studied the video, she tapped her finger on the tip of her nose. "Fast forward at double speed."

I watched in awe as the video instantly obeyed her command. Little squiggle lines bounced around as the video showed the entire morning at double the speed.

"There! Computer, pause video!" Maddie said, pointing at the screens. "Sophia is dropping the capsule off in the garbage can."

I stared at the frozen image of Sophia standing next to the garbage can. The timestamp on the video said it was 8:23 AM, which meant it was between homeroom and first period. It was clear that she had dug up the capsule before school, but didn't deliver it until *after* the school discovered it was missing. On the paused screen, I could see a hallway filled with students walking to their next class.

"She dumped it in front of a hallway of kids!" I said. "That's *crazy.*"

"*Bold* is more like it," Maddie said. "Computer, continue fast forwarding at double speed."

As the timestamp fast-forwarded, I felt my heart start to race. This was it. We were about to see Christopher Moss, A.K.A. *Christmas*, snatch the capsule from the garbage can – the last bit of evidence I'd need to clear my name. Sophia and Christopher would *both* get ˙ted and I'd be free to go back to living my boring little ˙ble life.

˙d then everything I knew to be true spit in my

Maddie and I stared at the television screens, our jaws dropped open, totally in shock of what we were watching.

"Computer," Maddie managed to whisper. "Play video at normal speed."

On the screen was a boy, digging through the garbage. He was facing away from the camera. Every time he looked over his shoulder, I had to squint to make sure I was actually seeing things straight. "That's not..." I whispered, but trailed off.

"It is," Maddie said. "It's Linus."

The video played on. My brain was jumping hurdles trying to understand what was happening. Linus pulled out the garbage can, dug his hands around the bottom, and removed the time capsule. He had a nervous look upon his face as he glanced over his shoulder every couple seconds.

"What's he doing with it?" I asked.

Maddie's voice was cold. "I don't know, but we're gonna find out."

I watched as Linus dropped the capsule into his backpack and shut the garbage can. But before he disappeared off camera, he stopped right in front of it, staring into it for an uncomfortably long time, as if he was surprised that it was even there. As an agent, shouldn't he know where *all* the cameras are?

"Computer," Maddie said as she spun her chair. "Resume normal recording."

The televisions all blinked again like they did before. One by one, each monitor flipped back to the video feed of whichever camera they were attached to.

I wasn't sure what was next. "What now?" I asked.

Maddie snapped to her feet, pushing the swivel chair away with the backs of her knees. "I don't know, okay? I don't have all the answers so quit bugging me for them!"

I lowered my gaze, embarrassed. "I'm sorry… I just…"

Maddie pushed me aside and stepped through the door. "Would you just keep your mouth shut? Just let me think for a second!"

Standing in the doorway, I didn't say another word.

Maddie paced back and forth in the hallway, occasionally picking her head up and looking at the camera that had caught Linus. Mumbling nonsense under her breath, she shook her head as if she were arguing with herself.

At last, she stopped and made eye contact with me. "We're gonna go straight to Suckerpunch."

"What about Linus?" I asked.

Maddie folded her arms tightly and tapped her foot, annoyed. "There's no point in trying to find him. We could look at his locker for clues, but there won't be any. He's too good to leave behind any evidence."

"But he left that video," I said.

"Whatever," Maddie said. "If Linus switched teams and is working for Suckerpunch, then he'll be there with the time capsule."

"What if he *didn't* switch teams?" I asked, trying to remain hopeful.

"Doesn't matter!" Maddie said. "Either way, he'll be with Suckerpunch right now, which means he'll have *a lot* of explaining to do. What period are we in again?"

I thought for a moment, and then answered. "We're halfway through third period now."

Maddie placed her hands on her hips and nodded. "We've only got a period and a half until lunch and that ridiculous school play about the football werewolf or whatever. I thought we'd have the case solved by then, but it doesn't seem to look that way."

I leaned against the lockers feeling that same sick feeling in my stomach as I thought about going to

71

Christmas himself. "Great," I said. "So where's Suckerpunch?"

"I don't know," Maddie said. "They've been one step ahead of Glitch when it comes to their hideout. Every time we think we've found them, they're not there. And they're snooty about it too, almost like they're kickin' back and relaxin' about the fact that we can't find them."

I paused. "What did you just say?"

"I said we don't know where their hideout is."

"No, the part after that. You said something about kickin' back and relaxin.' It's funny because when those monitors were taking me away earlier, I had the exact same thought," I said, trying to remember *why* I thought that. "What did they say?"

Maddie stared at me, holding her open palms out. "How would I know what you said?"

And then it came back to me, flashing across my mind. "It was when I was in the maintenance room! Someone said they forgot the key to the room back at the pool, and I thought it was *weird* 'cause Buchanan School doesn't *have* a pool!"

Maddie's eyes glistened as a smiled spread apart on her face. "But it *used* to."

Like the cool kid I was, I remained calm, and replied with, "Huh?"

"Buchanan School *used* to have a swimming pool," Maddie explained. "The rumor is that it got shut down back in the 90s because it was never cleaned or something. So they drained it and closed off that section of the school. It's mostly used for storage now I think. The entrance is *in* the gym. There are a set of double doors with a 'do not enter' sign taped to the wood."

The light bulb clicked on in my head. "You're right! And that actually makes a *ton* of sense. At least it explains why the boy's locker room always smells like steamed broccoli."

"That whole *area* smells like steamed broccoli," Maddie said, frowning. "So gross."

I followed Maddie to the edge of the stairs. Before she took a step, she looked back at me with her big brown eyes. "Are you ready for this?"

Was she kidding? After the morning I'd already had, I just wanted to go home and play some video games with a steaming cup of hot chocolate! Of course I wasn't ready for this, and I'm almost positive that I'd *never* be ready, but I couldn't bring myself to look away from her *humongous* brown eyes! Her eyelids fluttered and her good looks got the better of me. I grinned like an idiot, and said, "I was *born* ready."

Nearly ten minutes later, we were sneaking around the side of the gym, using the technique my dad taught me. The gym teacher, Mr. Cooper, even gave us a nod when we walked in front of his office. He either thought we were in his third period gym class, or he didn't care.

"Coach Cooper has that earring now," Maddie said. "Is that weird?"

73

"Very," I said. "He's an old dude. He shouldn't be getting his ears pierced. I mean, I *guess* he shouldn't. Who am I to say?"

"Still," Maddie said. "It's just the one tiny gold hoop, like he *wanted* to look like a pirate, but couldn't afford anything larger."

"Couldn't afford it?" I asked. "He's a *gym teacher.* That means he's loaded with money, doesn't it? Don't they make *tons* of money?"

Maddie frowned. "I don't know."

"Well, when I grow up, I know what I'll be spending all *my* money on."

"What's that?"

"Comic books," I said. "You know how many comics I'd have if I spent my yearly salary on them?"

Maddie didn't say anything.

"A lot," I said, answering for her, but instantly felt like a dork. Out of embarrassment, I tightened a smile and repeated myself. "I'd have *a lot.*"

The rest of the walk though the gymnasium was silent between us. I hoped it was because the situation we were walking into was one to be nervous about, and not because I embarrassed myself only seconds ago.

"Brody!" came a voice from behind me.

My heart dropped, afraid we were caught, but when I turned around, I saw that it wasn't anyone to be worried about. It was my friend, Chase. He had the same last name as Coach Cooper, but I was pretty they weren't related.

"You're definitely *not* in this class," Chase said, smiling and pointing at me.

"Uhhhh," I said, trying to come up with something clever.

"We're here on business," Maddie said flatly.

Chase smiled. "Hi," he said, holding out his hand. "My name's Chase."

"I know who you are," Maddie said as she took his hand, shaking it like a businesswoman. "But more importantly, I know *what* you are."

Chase's smile melted away as he continued to shake Maddie's hand. I wasn't sure what Maddie had meant by saying she knew *what* Chase was. Apparently he had some sort of secret. Maybe when this whole ordeal was over, I'd ask him about it.

Maddie's stiff face cracked, and she chuckled. "You have nothing to worry about," she said to Chase. "I know you're one of the few good guys at this school."

Yeah, I was definitely going to have to remember to ask him about Maddie's comment.

"Thanks," Chase said, looking rather uncomfortable. He turned his attention to me and spoke, worried. "So what's up, man? I saw that news report this morning on the television… was it… you?"

"No!" I said, louder than I meant to. "That's actually what we're doing here. We think we've found the person behind the whole thing."

Chase furrowed his brow. "*Behind* the whole thing? What do you mean?"

I knew I said too much. I always did whenever I was nervous. "It's nothing," I said as cool as possible, scratching the back of my neck. "I just mean that we're trying to help them find it."

"Who's them?" Chase asked.

"Why all the questions, Chase?" is what I *wanted* to yell, but instead I just shrugged my shoulders. "Y'know… *them.*"

Another voice cracked from across the room. "There he is! Brody Valentine, stop right in your tracks!"

Chase spun around. "What? You're still running?"

"Dude, you gotta believe me," I pleaded. "I swear it wasn't me that took the time capsule!"

Maddie stepped forward. "Brody's innocent, and we're about to bust the guys behind it, but we need some time."

Chase's eyes grew fierce. He nodded once. "Go," he said. "Quickly before those monitors get over here. I'll hold them off as long as I can."

I tightened a smile at him. Chase was a good kid, but even more, I considered him an actual friend. "Thanks," I said.

"Thank me when this is over," Chase said, turning around.

Maddie started sprinting to the far end of the gym, to the double doors with the "do not enter" sign. I ran as quickly as I could, looking back at Chase every few seconds. He was able to distract a few of the covert monitors by running circles around them, but the rest of the monitors were still coming after Maddie and me.

"Faster!" Maddie shouted.

I was feeling good, running like a cheetah across the gym floor up until my side cramped up on me. It hurt so bad that I stumbled.

Maddie pushed open the double doors that supposedly led to the abandoned swimming pool and Suckerpunch's hideout. She turned and reached her hand out to me. "Come on, Brody!"

Hobbling, I did my best to keep my pace.

"Stop right there, Brody!" the monitor shouted.

Most of the kids in the gymnasium were staring at that point, watching to see if a fight was going to break out. I was trying my best to keep it from coming to that.

"Grab my hand!" Maddie shouted one last time.

I choked down my pain and launched myself forward at the double doors. Maddie caught my wrist and pulled me into the next room through the doors. Instantly, she sprang up and pushed the doors shut. Grabbing an old broom, she wedged it between the handles of the double doors, locking it.

The monitor on the other side slammed into the door with all his force, but the broom didn't budge. His muffled voice came filtered through the cracks. "You can't run forever, Valentine!"

Rolling to my feet, I arched my back as I stood up, trying to stretch out the cramp in my side. I listened as the monitor jumped into the doors again. He was a big kid, and I was surprised that the broom wasn't breaking.

"We'd better hurry," Maddie said as she walked across the floor.

The room we were in was just an entrance to an entrance. It was the area where people would gather to pay for a ticket to see the swim competition.

On the far right wall was a huge boarded up window that probably served hot dogs and soda back when Buchanan used to have swim meets. On the far left was a bench against a wall where pictures of swimmers hung. At the end of each side, there was an opening in the brick wall that probably led to the boy's and girl's locker rooms. I never noticed a sealed door from inside the locker room, but I bet I'd find it if I looked.

And at the far end of the room, directly in front of Maddie and me, was another set of double doors. The words "Buchanan Swimming Pool" was painted on the frosted glass portion of each door.

"There it is," I said, taking the lead.

"Wait," Maddie said, snatching my elbow.

I turned around. "What?"

"I didn't really think this through," Maddie admitted with a shaky voice. She reached into her pocket and pulled out a red object. Holding it out at me, she said, "Here. Take this. It's my last one. It's a custom smoke shell – no need to light anything. Just pull the string on the end of it to pop it open, and slam it on the ground as hard as you can. The chalk dust will burst from it, creating a smoke screen…y'know, in case you need it. In case things go… *wrong.*"

Taking it in my fingers, I grinned. "More spy stuff. Cool." I paused, realizing neither of us had actually talked about a plan. "What if something *does* goes wrong?" I asked.

Maddie took a deep breath, and stepped past me. When she got to the second set of double doors, she looked at me, knocked on the glass, and said, "If something goes wrong, follow the raven."

Follow the raven? Was she talking about Linus's business card he gave me last week? Before I could ask, the double doors cracked open an inch.

A voice from the other side hissed. "Happy holidays."

Maddie shot me a look, totally confused. She paused, lifting her hands up toward me and shrugging her shoulders. She wasn't sure how to respond. "Ummm….."

"Happy holidays," the voice said again, a little more gruff.

"I don't know what he's talking about," Maddie mouthed to me.

And then I remembered that earlier in the day, I had heard one of the covert monitors say the exact same thing. It had to be a code they used to make sure they were dealing with other Suckerpunch agents! I jumped forward and nearly squealed. "I prefer the term 'Merry Christmas!'"

There was silence as Maddie and I stared at each other. Had I said the right thing? Were we busted? Was my side going to cramp up again from another chase? I hoped not, because I wasn't sure I could handle it another time.

Finally, the door creaked open. The boy on the other side was hidden in the shadows. I heard him breathing heavily, as if he were a chubby kid that just finished running the mile. And then I realized that it was *me* that was doing the heavy breathing. The Suckerpunch doorkeeper didn't say a thing as he waved us in, allowing us to enter their base of operations.

I wish I could tell you that it was a room filled with awesome spy gear and agents training with crazy science fiction stuff, but I'm sad to say it wasn't that at all. Instead, it looked exactly how an abandoned swimming pool would look if sixth graders were seated around it looking at their laptops and cell phones. It looked like a LAN party, where each kid was playing the same videogame with each other, but on different screens. And if you've ever seen a LAN party, then you'd know there wasn't anything exciting about it unless you were actually playing one of the games.

"How disappointing," I said.

"I promise Glitch has a cooler base," Maddie said. She held her arm out, and whispered. "Look!"

Not even five feet away, the time capsule was resting on a rickety table, right next to us. I was so excited that I had to keep myself from jumping at it. Curling my toes in my shoes, I grit my teeth, and whispered softly. "Let's just grab it and go before we're caught."

Maddie acted like she didn't hear me. She stepped farther into the room with determination as if she knew exactly where she was going. When her walk turned into a run, I knew she was after something, and I knew it was only seconds before the Suckerpunch agents saw that we were there. "Linus, you traitor!" she shouted as her feet stomped on the concrete.

Across the room, I saw Linus jump up from a table. On the other side of the table, I saw the figure of another sixth grader who I've only seen in passing between classes. It was Christopher Moss, or as I've come to know him, Christmas.

"You're so dead!" Maddie shouted like a warrior as she dodged enemy agents that dove after her.

My knees felt weak as I watched her run away, shrinking against the backdrop of the abandoned room. I wanted so badly to run after her because I *knew* she was going to be in trouble in just a second, but the time capsule kept screaming for attention on the table beside me. The agent covering the door ran after Maddie, leaving the exit *and* the capsule unguarded.

"Forget it!" I grunted as I snatched the time capsule. I stuck my arm through the strap and pulled it up to my shoulder. The sounds of footsteps echoed across the empty concrete of the pool as I darted back to the exit.

Slipping through the door unnoticed, I leaned against the wall, listening to the door click shut. Maddie screamed at Linus, her muffled voice vibrating against the frosted glass until spilling into the room I was hiding in. I felt terrible.

But I did my best to shake the feeling of abandoning Maddie off my shoulders. Now that I had the capsule on my shoulder, I couldn't waste any time wondering if I could help her. She was a highly trained secret agent! She could handle herself, right?

I heard her muted shout one last time. "Follow the raaaaaven!"

I balled my fists out of frustration, knowing that she was telling me what to do, but I also knew it was only a matter of seconds before Suckerpunch's agents realized the time capsule was gone. I had to act fast.

The hall monitor in the gymnasium was still pounding against the double doors so that exit was blocked off. I wondered if Chase was still doing his best to keep the other monitors occupied. I slipped into entrance to the boy's locker room instead, hoping there wasn't a sealed door. Lucky for me, there wasn't.

I was beginning to really appreciate how many exits there were to boy's locker room. I was able to bypass the gymnasium completely and jump right into the hallway of the school, near the lobby.

I stood in silence as more thoughts bounced around my noggin. Was there anything I could change about what just happened? I sighed, knowing the answer was that I probably shouldn't have run out on Maddie. My guilt sunk like a brick in my stomach.

At that moment, the bell rang. Third period was over and students were about to pour out of their classrooms. My face was still plastered all over the walls of the school so there wasn't any chance that I could stay invisible. Was this how super cool kids felt? Like they couldn't go anywhere without people knowing who they were?

Shoving the time capsule under the front of my shirt, I moved to a water fountain and stepped on the pedal at the bottom. Water began shooting out of the spout as I bent over to take small sips. The ice-cold liquid made my teeth hurt as I listened to students walk by me, engaged in their daily gossip.

"Did you hear they haven't caught Brody yet?"

"I heard he escaped the school and flew the coop! Headed to Mexico or something. Hope he knows how to speak Spanish."

"Did they ever find the time capsule he took? What was in it?"

"I don't think they did. I heard it was filled with millions of dollars worth of pirate treasure though – probably how he could afford to escape the country."

I kept sipping the water. Did they really just suggest that the time capsule was filled with pirate treasure? My classmates at Buchanan weren't exactly the smartest bunch, I'll be the first to admit that.

"Hurry up, man!" said a boy behind me as he nudged my foot with his own.

I slurped at the water and coughed because I

accidentally inhaled some. Covering my mouth, I managed to squeeze out a "sorry" before stumbling down the hall. Another kid bumped into me, tossing me back toward the fountain. After a few more steps, I found myself in the middle of the hallway, deep in the flowing river of students.

I kept my hand over my face as I coughed, but after I noticed that I was getting *more* attention from coughing, I stopped. If I kept covering my face, it would've looked weird so I stared at the ground instead and stopped trying to walk *against* the crowd.

After a few steps, I found myself swept up by the rush of kids. They weren't even paying attention to me! Keeping my head down, I walked as if I were going to my next class. A wave of cold air washed over my body and my walk suddenly felt very familiar. I sighed with each step, feeling a numbness in my limbs, like I was an undead zombie walking the halls.

The time capsule remained under my shirt the entire time. Both my hands were on it, making sure it stayed that way.

As I marched with the other students, I remember the last thing Maddie said to me. *Follow the raven.* She was obviously talking about the raven on the business card Linus handed me the week before, but the business card was still in my wallet, and only the monitors at Buchanan knew where *that* was at.

Good thing I had it memorized.

I'll confess it wasn't hard to memorize. It was just a business card with an inkblot of a black raven with the numbers 17 and 4 written in roman numerals under it. The problem was that I didn't know what the raven *or* the numbers meant.

But wait... *why* was I even bothering with the time capsule anymore? Why not just take it to the principal's office and be done with the horrible day I've had? Maddie was *probably* going to be fine. Sure, she was with Suckerpunch now, but that was just a group of sixth graders. What were they gonna do?

...what *were* they gonna do? I felt my stomach turn as I imagined them cutting Maddie's hair or something.

No way. Linus wouldn't let them do that. Linus might be fighting for the bad guys now, but Maddie was still his friend... wasn't she?

The truth was that I had no clue. About *any* of it, and it was getting on my nerves so bad that I didn't even notice that my hands were stinging from the kung fu grip I had on the time capsule through my shirt.

The right thing was to help Maddie. I *knew* it was the right thing because my stomach settled down as soon as I made the decision to do it. For the second time in my life, I had to make the decision to do the *right* thing instead of the *safe* thing.

And I felt alive again.

I snuck a peak at the time on one of the clocks on the wall, trying to see how much longer I had until fourth period started. I was in the lobby of the school where there was a clock hanging above the tinted cafeteria windows, and two other clocks at opposite ends of each other, hanging above the east hallway and the west hallway.

The clock I checked was above the west hallway, but for some reason, I glanced back at the clock above the cafeteria. I'm not sure why – maybe something in my brain told me to do it – maybe it was a coincidence. But when I did, I saw a familiar image.

The logo on the bottom part of the cafeteria clock was a symbol in the shape of a raven. When I checked the west hallway clock again, the raven logo *wasn't* on it. Of course, I naturally spun in place and looked at the east end clock. I wasn't surprised to see that the raven *wasn't* there either.

Follow the raven.

Alright, Maddie. I hope you knew what you were doing. I sifted my way through the other students until I made it to the cafeteria doors. Through the glass, I saw the drama team setting up for the play that was supposed to be performed during lunch, the one about the werewolf football player.

I opened the door, and snuck into the cafeteria, keeping as close to the wall as possible. The black sheets were still draped on coat hangers just like earlier that morning so it was like walking into a maze, which was great because I didn't have to worry about being spotted.

The only thing I could see was the area above the black sheets, but that's all I *needed* to see. I looked for another clock and was surprised to find two of them in there. One was directly above the stage, and didn't have a raven. The other clock was placed above the kitchen doors.

And that one *did* have the raven logo.

I won't lie. I had a goofy smile on my face. Wouldn't you? I was super excited about finding the path!

Creeping against the wall, I kept myself outside of the maze of black sheets. There wasn't much sense in trying to find the way through the maze rather than around it. When I got to the kitchen doors, I paused to collect my thoughts.

What was going to happen when I found the Glitch headquarters? Would they even listen to me? What if they locked me away in detention forever? I shook my head. No. I wasn't going to stand in my own way this time. Maddie was in trouble. Linus was a traitor. I had to get in there and just tell everyone what I saw. They were agents and they'd be able to handle it from here.

I pushed down on the handle and opened the door, proudly taking another step into the unexpected.

The kitchen lights were switched off, but the stainless steel shelving had a glow that illuminated enough of the room for me to see. I carefully walked over the polished flooring, my shoes squeaking with each step.

A shadow suddenly rose up from behind me. I nearly jumped out of my skin as I fell against one of the shelves. I was afraid for my life until I figured out it was just my eyes playing tricks on me. The thin slit from the kitchen doors allowed a small amount of light into the room. Because of that light, shadows loomed and danced all around me.

I turned around and scanned the clock above the inside of the kitchen doors. No raven.

As I stepped farther into the room, I saw an object twinkling near the back of the room where it was the darkest. Squinting, I allowed my eyes to adjust a little more and could see the faint outline of a circle. It was another clock, glinting at me like it was trying to get my attention so I slid over the counter to see what it wanted.

I had to put my face right up to the clock to see it clearly in the dark. On the bottom portion, I saw the same logo of the raven that the other clocks had. A smooth metal door was standing next to the clock, and on the other side was a glowing number pad. The roman numerals must've been the code I had to punch into the pad.

I smiled. "Like candy from baby," I whispered.

"But candy from a baby is bad and um… what I'm doing is good. Uh… like *giving* candy to a baby – no wait, that's probably not a good thing either. Whatever."

I stopped messing around and punched the numbers into the pad. It beeped after every digit.

"One…"

Beep.

"Seven…"

Beep.

"Four…"

Beep.

After the last beep, the number pad blinked red and white. I heard a rush of air as the smooth stainless steel door sunk back an inch before sliding open. I took another breath, and stepped through the door to the Glitch headquarters.

Just like the rest of my morning, what I saw disappointed me. I walked into a massive room, but there was *nothing* inside. It was just an empty room with a bunch of empty desks. To be fair, it *looked* like something *used* to be in the room.

I was about to turn around and give up until I heard the sound of slow clapping echo off the glossy walls. I'm not the kind of kid that enjoys surprises, especially when it involves being alone in an empty room made of brushed metal. I've seen enough horror movies to imagine how these situations end.

Spinning in place, I dashed back to the open door of the kitchen, but I was too late. There were two boys blocking my path, staring at me with their arms folded. They weren't dressed as covert monitors. The only other thing I could think of was that they were agents of Suckerpunch.

I stared through the two boys, listening to the slow clapping that continued. I shut my eyes and shook my head. Way to go, Brody. You just walked into a trap. I turned around to see who was on the other side of the room, but as I did, I already knew it was Christopher Moss. *Christmas.*

Christmas laughed and clapped one final time. "If it isn't Mr. Brody Valentine himself!"

"Christopher Moss," I hissed.

"Oh, come on," Christmas said. His voice was a little higher than you'd expect from a super sixth grader. He sounded the way someone does when they're joyful.

"Only my friends call me *Christopher*. My enemies call me *Christmas*. I guess we're about to find out which name *you'd* like to call me."

CHRISTOPHER MOSS AKA CHRISTMAS

Placing my hand on my chin, I cracked my neck. "I got a couple names I'd like to call ya."

Christmas stopped in place. He pressed his lips together and wagged a scolding finger at me. "Nice burn," he said. "But you seem to forget who has the power in this room."

At that moment, one of his bodyguards behind me kicked at the back of my knee. I lost my balance and dropped to the cold metal floor. I tightened a smile as I tried to pretend it didn't hurt. The time capsule slipped out from under my shirt, but I caught it just before it hit the floor.

Christmas frowned. "*That's* what you *get* when you run your mouth. Can we try this again, but without the sass?"

Staring at the floor, I didn't speak.

"I see you have the time capsule," Christmas said joyfully, pointing at the container in my hands. "I won't even take the thing away from you, alright? This will be a *peaceful* conversation."

"Where's Maddie?" I asked coldly.

"She's been...," Christmas paused, folding his arms. "*Dealt* with."

"If you hurt her in any—"

Christmas put his hands up and patted at the air. "She's *fine* for now, alright?"

I didn't answer.

Christmas's dress shoes clopped on the floor as he restarted his walk. "Even a quiet guy like you has to admit that today has been pretty fun, no?"

Still on my knees, I stared at the floor, making sure I didn't make eye contact with him. If he used to be part of Glitch, then I knew I had to work extra hard at hiding my fear.

Christmas held his arms out and spun in a circle. "Do you like what I've done with the place?" His laugh bounced off the metal walls. "This room used to be filled with pests, but I think I've done a bang up job of clearing them out!"

"So Glitch *used* to be here?" I asked.

Christmas curled the side of his lip, trying to form what I thought was a smile. "Correct. They *used* to be here," he growled. Then with his high-pitched voice, he laughed. "I guess they got *spooked* or something, right? And all I wanted to do was say hello, but by the time I got here this afternoon, they had already packed up. Headed south like a bunch of ugly ducks afraid of the cold weather that Christmas brings."

Ew. Was this boy really going to use his name as a pun?

Christmas continued to speak. He was a smooth talker, that much was for sure, but he was also very animated in the way he gestured with his hands when he talked. With his fingers pressed together, he almost danced as he made his way toward me. "It's really a shame you didn't see this place when it was at its prime, *last* year."

I chuckled. "That's right. I almost forgot you enjoyed sixth grade so much you decided to come back for seconds."

Christmas's face flushed with red. I heard one of the bodyguards move behind me again so I braced for another kick, but Christmas snapped his hand out and shook his head. It was his way of ordering the bodyguard to back down. He had power, and he knew how to use it.

I watched as Christmas took a deep breath and cracked his knuckles. I really hoped he wasn't thinking of introducing his fists to my face. My nose can't talk, but if it could I bet it'd say something like, "I really enjoy not being broken!"

"Brody," Christmas said softly. "What's your role in all this?"

I paused, confused. "What do you mean?"

Christmas smiled as if he felt sorry for me. "Your *purpose*," he repeated. "Why are you even here? What are you looking for?"

Still unsure of what Christmas meant, I said, "I was looking for the Glitch headquarters. Duh."

Christmas let out a small laugh. "But *why*? Is it because you think you're secret agent material?"

"It's because—," I started to answer, but he interrupted me.

"Is it because you're crushing on Maddie?" Christmas said. "Maybe you think all this is going to mean you guys will go out someday?"

"No," I said, my voice cracking.

"Then what?" Christmas asked. "Surely it's not because you think you're Glitch material because you'd make a *terrible* agent."

His words cut like a knife. I didn't think I had crazy awesome spy skills, but I *was* beginning to think I was *sorta* good at this. Was it possible I was utterly wrong? Maybe. It's happened before.

"I can see that doubt in your eyes," Christmas said, finally standing before me. "I look at you, and I can tell you're the kind of kid that *doesn't* crave adventure. Am I right?"

"Maybe."

"And yet here are you in the middle of one. Trouble *found* you, didn't it?" Christmas asked, holding his open hand out to me. I think he wanted me to shake it.

"…maybe," I replied, ignoring his outstretched hand.

Clasping his hand shut, Christmas drew it back. "Listen carefully, Mr. Valentine, because I'll only offer this once."

I rose from the floor, feeling the weight of the time capsule in my palms.

"Join us," Christmas hissed. "Join Suckerpunch. You've shown that you want *more* in life, but Glitch isn't going to get you anywhere anytime soon. I can't say that Suckerpunch will get you there quicker, but what I *can* tell you is that Suckerpunch promises to bring chaos to Buchanan School. Complete and utter chaos."

"You created Suckerpunch just to cause trouble?" I asked.

"I spent all of last year trying to bring peace and keep things safe," Christmas said. "But safe is *boring*. I think this time around, I'll introduce a little *madness*."

Safe is boring. Funny how Maddie said the same thing to me.

Christmas continued his rant. "After all, Glitch has *abandoned* you! Instead of helping you today, they've tucked their tails between their legs and buried themselves in a hole somewhere, leaving you completely on your own to deal with one of *their* problems – *me*."

"That's not true," I said.

Christmas hopped backward, acting shocked. Raising his eyebrows, he opened his arms up and waved them at the empty desks. "Do you *see* them? Because I sure don't!" His shoulders sunk as he turned to face me. "Are they just voices? Do the voices tell you to do things, Brody? Do they keep you awake at night?"

"I don't hear voices," I said, annoyed. I wasn't sure if Christmas wanted me to like him or hate him. He was nuts! Impossible to read!

Out of nowhere, Christmas dropped to the floor and crossed his legs, rocking back and forth like a child waiting to open presents. "You were like a flame to a moth," he murmured. "A *fish* that couldn't resist the bait."

I narrowed my eyes, watching the super sixth grader on the floor. "Bait?"

Christmas clapped rapidly, excited by his own words. "You're predictable, Brody Valentine! A predictable sixth grader that did exactly as I wanted you to! Of course I have to give myself a *little* credit, after all, it was *my* genius brain that made the plan. Boy, if my brain could scream gleefully, it totally would!"

I shook my head. I was beginning to feel embarrassed, but I wasn't sure why. "What are you talking about? *I've* got the time capsule now. You've lost! My name is as good as cleared!"

Without warning, Christmas sprang to his feet and screamed like a maniac. "*Look around you, Valentine!* You're on your *own* now! Glitch isn't around for you to *hide* behind, *is* it? You're just a *nobody* that the whole school thinks is a thief!"

"But when I return the capsule, I'll tell them what you've done, and what you're *planning* on doing!" I shouted.

"Who's going to believe a *thief?*" Christmas replied. "You really think Principal Davis is going to believe you if you waltz into his office and return the time capsule he thinks *you* stole! Yeah, right," Christmas said nodding, rolling his eyes and tossing me a thumbs-up. "Good luck with all *that*."

I could feel my blood boiling again.

Christmas spoke to me like he was scolding a child. "You really goofed up this time, didn't ya? Getting Sophia to set you up was the hardest part of this whole thing, but as soon as you took the bait, the dominoes all fell over perfectly. You escaped from the covert monitors in the morning and created your own mission to find the capsule. I just had to dangle it far enough for you that you couldn't resist the challenge of finding it."

"You're insane," I whispered.

Christmas grinned and continued his monologue. "When Sophia was caught, I *knew* she'd rat me out to Glitch. Being a member of Glitch last year, I also knew they'd see me as more of a threat than they had before. I didn't expect them to move their base so quickly," Christmas said, spinning in a circle, "but as you can see, they sure did! Glitch is running around like a chicken with its head cut off! Plus the amazing Brody Valentine will be locked away in detention until college, and *I* got what I wanted from the time capsule."

I swallowed hard, feeling a knot in my throat. He just said he got what he wanted from the capsule. Had my entire morning been a waste of time? If I could go back and change things, I totally would've followed Linus so I could've caught him when he took the capsule from the garbage can. Blast!

"Check out the best part," Christmas said, laughing and patting at the air again. "That time capsule has *your* finger prints all over it. You're done, Brody. I've *won*."

He was right. Even as he laughed, I was rolling the capsule around with my fingers, which is where most fingerprints are located, just sayin'. I could've tried tossing it at Christmas, but he'd stay away from it like it had cooties.

Christmas stepped past me and mumbled some words to his bodyguards. I stood in place with my fingers aching from the heavy time capsule. What was I going to do? What *could* I do?

The two bodyguards were blocking the exit to the kitchen. Christmas had entered the room somewhere on the other side, but there was no way I could tell if he had other bodyguards stationed there.

Christmas thinks he's giving me a choice by offering me a place in Suckerpunch, but what he didn't know was that it was *never* an option for me. Linus was the one that said if I was going to do the right thing, I'd have to do the right thing *no matter what*. In that moment, I became a firm believer of that, even if the person who said it had chosen the *wrong* thing.

As slowly as possible, I reached into the front pocket of my jeans and felt the smoke shell that Maddie had given me earlier. Easing it out, I held it in my palm. Just as I was about to yank on the string, I overheard the conversation Christmas was having with his bodyguards.

"Hand me the CD, please," Christmas's voice snipped.

Both of the bodyguards mumbled back and forth to each other until one of them finally said, "Uh, boss, we thought *you* had it."

Christmas's voice became a whisper. *"What are you talking about? I told you to remove it from the time* capsule back at headquarters. Remember? I said take the CD out and put the capsule on the table by the door! *Now which one of you has the CD?*"

"Not me," the first bodyguard said.

The other spoke softly. "Me neither."

"You mean…," Christmas sighed. "*The disc is still in the capsule?*"

I took that as a sign for me to set off the smoke shell. Clutching the small object in my hand, I pulled the string apart from the other end. I did as Maddie had instructed and slammed it into the floor by my feet. A blast of white chalk dust swallowed the entire room. I dove forward to gain speed, making sure I made a ton of noise so Christmas knew I was trying to escape.

"After him!" shouted Christmas's voice.

I rolled over one of the desks and stood perfectly

still in the thick cloud, listening as the two bodyguards and Christmas ran right past me without a clue. Their heavy footsteps led away until I couldn't hear them anymore.

As the dust thinned out, I spun around to savor the fact that I had fooled those bullies, but apparently I was too quick to celebrate. I was wrong – Christmas was still in the room, staring right at me.

With fire in his eyes, he shouted. "Give me the time capsule, Brody!"

Spinning in place, I dashed for the other end of the room. Wonderful, I thought. At some point, those two bodyguards were going to realize I wasn't in front of them and turn around, which meant I'd be completely surrounded.

The entrance on the other end of the room came into view and was wide open. Jumping through the doorway, I found myself in what looked like a back alley, but with a ceiling over the top. Metal pipes stretched down both walls on either side of me with breaks in the places where other corridors met the one we were in.

The walls became a blur as I raced through the narrow hallway. I could hear Christmas's footsteps and shouts behind me, but I never bothered looking back. All I wanted to do was get to safety without smashing my face against one of the brick walls.

Faster and faster I ran, cutting sharp corners and tearing my way through the hidden back section of Buchanan School. I had a firm grip around the time capsule, keeping it close to my body. After a minute of sprinting, I glanced behind me to see that I was alone, but I continued to run in a circle of confusion until I was absolutely sure Christmas wasn't on my tail anymore.

Catching my breath, I studied the concrete walls, trying to make sense of where I was in the school. Without a map or anything, it was impossible for me to tell. All I knew was that I was somewhere *way* behind the kitchen.

Feeling the stress of what little time I had left, I started jogging down the corridor through the humid air, passing small openings that looked like offices for the maintenance people.

"Brody!" shouted a girl's voice just as I ran past one of the openings.

I slid to a stop and spun around excited. When I walked into the small office, I saw Maddie. She was sitting on a chair, but wasn't tied down or anything.

"What gives?" I asked. "How come you're sitting back here?"

Maddie jumped to her feet and threw her arms around me. "Christmas told me that if I waited here, then he'd bring you back so we could all talk it out!"

"And you *believed* him?" I asked, confused. Nodding my head, I tightened a smirk. "No, I get it. That kid's a smooth talker, isn't he? I would've believed him too."

"You have the capsule!" Maddie said.

I held up the container. "Yep."

"Did he say why he wanted it? What's inside that thing?"

Poking my head into the corridor, I checked to make sure we were still alone. "No, he never said why he wanted this. What about Linus? What happened back there?"

Maddie shrugged her shoulders. "I dunno," she grunted. "Those Suckerpunch goons got to me before I could get to him."

"Mega bummer," I said.

"It is," Maddie said, taking the lead down the corridor. "Come on. The exit's down this way."

Maddie's wristwatch chirped loudly, and then Christmas's voice came through. "Hello there, Maddie," Christmas said over the tiny speaker. "I'm sure Brody is with you by now so would you be a doll and give him this message for me? Tell him I'd like that time capsule back, please and thank you."

Maddie jogged up to a metal door and pushed down on the handle. The carpeted hallway of the school was right on the other side. "Don't listen to him," Maddie said. "It's time we went straight to Principal Davis with it."

The wristwatch chirped again. "Tsk, tsk, tsk," Christmas scolded. "The two of you are being very *very* naughty! Now bring me that time capsule, or *else*."

Maddie stopped in the open door. "Or else *what?*"

"This," Christmas said.

Immediately, the school's fire alarm blasted overhead. The horn was so loud that I covered my ears in pain. I could see Maddie say something to me, but I couldn't hear her.

Classroom doors flipped open as students filed out of the rooms. Because the fire alarm was activated, every single person in the school had to make their way outside.

Just when I thought my luck couldn't get worse, I saw a team of covert monitors stop in their tracks and point at me. One of them put his finger to his ear and spoke, probably alerting all the other monitors that I was spotted.

Maddie pushed me back through the door. The fire alarm was still going off, but it wasn't as loud in there. "There's a ladder to the roof back in that room I was waiting in! Get to the roof! I'll hold the monitors back!"

"But what about you?" I cried.

"I'll be fine!" Maddie shouted. "Get to the roof!"

Once she pulled the door shut, I started racing back to the small office we had just walked out of. I wasn't looking forward to climbing a ladder all the way to the roof, but I was so freaked out that I wasn't thinking straight. It probably wasn't the smartest thing I'd ever done, but again, my brain was wonky.

The ladder was exactly where Maddie said it was. On the back wall of the small office, metal loops stuck out from the walls and reached through a small opening in the ceiling. I was thrilled to see that it wasn't just a wooden ladder resting against the wall, but a solid passage to the rooftop.

Securing the strap of the time capsule around my shoulder, I grabbed the first metal loop and started making my way up.

On the rooftop, I slid away from the opening I had climbed out of, letting the rusted hunk of metal fall back into place. I heard a dull clunk and knew that the opening had locked itself. So much for climbing back *down* the ladder.

I hopped to my feet, sliding against the loose gravel under my sneakers. When I got to the side of the building, I looked over the edge and saw that most of the students had gathered in the parking lot. A few of them noticed me, and pointed.

Flinching, I dropped to the ground and started crawling across the gravel. There had to be another way down, there just *had* to be! A door or another opening that was locked tight had to be *somewhere* up there.

And then I heard the sound of kids shouting at me, but it wasn't coming from the parking lot. It was coming from across the rooftop!

"Great," I groaned as I stared at what looked like *every* covert monitor at Buchanan gathering at the other end of the roof, spilling from of an open elevator behind them.

"Turn yourself in, Valentine!" shouted the lead monitor. "You've got nowhere to run!"

"Just my luck," I said, exhaling slowly. I rose to my feet, and made my way back to the edge.

There I was on the rooftop of the school, looking over the side of the building as the *entire* squad of the school's monitors closed in behind me. I glanced over my shoulder, trying to estimate how much time I had before they caught me. Ten seconds at best, I thought.

I was completely cornered without a single escape

option I could think of. I leaned my head over the edge and saw the grass two stories down. There were groups of students clumped together over most of the schoolyard and parking lot, staring and pointing fingers at me. The wind picked up and blew my hair around, making my stomach queasy.

Looking to the sky, I did my best to push the dizzy feeling out of my body. If I stared at the clouds or something, maybe I could trick myself into thinking I *wasn't* on the rooftop of my school.

And then I saw a small flock of birds flying in the distance, making me wish I had wings. They were black, like the raven logo I had searched for earlier. Seeing them somehow comforted me.

I gripped my hand around the canvas strap on my shoulder and pulled it tighter. The time capsule attached to the strap pressed against my shirt as it rose. The weight of the capsule surprised me. It was heavy – heavier than I expected, at least.

I took a breath, listening to the footsteps of a hundred hall monitors circle behind me. I know, right? *A hundred* monitors for *me*. Seems like a bit of an overkill for one kid…

But instead of being afraid, I smiled, confident that even a *hundred* of 'em couldn't stop me.

I remembered my dad's advice and imagined the monitors as old ladies trying to grab a handful of my face. I dug my shoes into the gravel, and bolted directly at them – I think it's called a "blitz" in football.

A few of the monitors panicked, diving out of the way. In all the confusion, the rest of the monitors stumbled about, trying to make sense of what was happening. I think they were trying to figure out if someone had grabbed me or not.

I felt a hand snatch the strap on my shoulder and jerk me to the ground, but I instantly dropped and rolled away from the monitor. My quick moves caused a couple other kids to jump over me to avoid getting hit.

Once I was clear, I jumped to my feet and continued to run right through the heart of the squadron of monitors. I couldn't believe it was working! My dad's advice was working! They were so confused that a bunch of them could only watch as I ran by them.

Finally, I emerged on the other side of monitors, totally surprised that I had gotten out with barely a scratch. Hobbling the last few feet, I entered the open doors of the elevator. I turned and pretended to tip my hat at the defeated monitors. "It's been fun, boys, but it's time we part ways," I said sarcastically as I punched the "G" button for "ground floor." The doors slid shut, and I was left in silence.

Smooth jazz flowed from the speakers as I caught my breath. The time capsule was still safe in my bag, and for the moment, I was safe too. The elevator ride was so calm and quiet that it almost felt like I was dreaming. I even found myself whistling along with the music as I watched the numbers above the door switch from "2" to "G." When the doors opened, I knew I'd be in the lobby of the school. That meant all I had to do was make it to the offices and this whole situation would be over with.

The elevator beeped as it came to a stop. Just before the doors slid apart, I felt a knot in my throat. If there were any other monitors that weren't on the rooftop, then it was possible that they'd be right on the other side of the doors. In all my excitement, I hadn't thought that part through.

When the doors opened, I wasn't surprised to see that the situation was worse that I thought – it always was. Christmas was standing there, and he looked furious.

"How perfect!" he sneered. "The universe has smiled upon me after all."

I was going to say something witty, but went with something a little more physical. Jumping from the elevator, I pushed against Christmas. As he tripped over his feet, I immediately leapt off to the side to keep him from grabbing me.

"Get back here!" he shouted as he reached his hand out.

His fingers brushed against my shirt as I barely slipped away. I saw the entrance of the front lobby not even ten yards away, but I knew I would never make it there with Christmas so close behind me, so in my panic, I took a hard right turn, jumping into the cafeteria.

I scampered across the floor, hoping I didn't fall over on any of the folding chairs. The drama team already had the room set up for the play they were putting on. The black sheets that were draped across curtain rods were near the stage, so I made my way toward them. If I could just get into the confusing maze, I thought maybe I'd have a shot at losing the psycho behind me.

I heard Christmas's footsteps clap across the floor just as I glided into the maze of sheets. Without paying any attention to what I was doing, I made my way down random paths and just hoped for the best.

I heard the heavy breathing of Christmas as he searched for me. "You can't run forever, Valentine! What do you really think is going to happen here?"

I remained silent.

Just then, the bell rang out with three short bursts. It was the signal for the end of the fire drill. Almost instantly, I heard the footsteps of students slap on the floor of the cafeteria. Since fourth period was just about over, everyone was gathering for the play instead of getting back to their classes.

I knew there was no way I'd make it out of the

cafeteria without getting caught so that idea was out. If only I could find my way to the back of the maze, I could probably sneak out that way.

Turning right, and then left, and then right again, I found myself more confused than when I started. I had no idea what direction I was facing, but then I remembered the clocks! If I could see which clock had the raven logo on it, I'd know where the kitchen was and all I'd have to do was go in the opposite direction!

At that moment, the lights in the cafeteria dimmed in preparation for the play. Even if I *could* still see the clocks, there's no way I'd be able to see a tiny raven logo without any light.

Frustrated, I began running through the maze, turning down any corner I came to. At that point, I didn't care if I jumped out in front of a thousand students. I just didn't want to get caught by Christmas.

I ran without thinking.

Turn left.

Turn right.

Turn left.

Turn left again…

Until I couldn't go any farther. The last turn brought me to a wonky looking wooden door with a metal sign that read "Boy's Locker Room Entrance 6B."

Finally, my luck was turning around. Again, I felt thankful for the fact that Buchanan's locker rooms had so many entrances. I pushed against the door, sliding it open slowly. The small rush of cold air felt good against my face as the opening split apart to reveal more of the locker room.

As I took my first step, I heard Christmas growl behind me. "Oh no you don't!"

Jumping into the dark room, I ran down a couple aisles, keeping on eye over my shoulder. The time capsule bounced on my back as I darted back and forth, trying to find a good hiding spot.

The door clicked shut, and all I heard was the sound of Christmas catching his breath. It reminded me of the type of horror movie where the bad guy was right around the corner.

Pushing myself against one of the cold metal lockers, I waited to see what he was going to do. My plan was to make sure I knew exactly where he was in the room before bolting back out into the lobby.

I stared at the spot above the lockers. The room was nearly pitch black except for a few spots that seemed to glow with yellow light. I'd never seen the boy's locker room like that before, but I've also never looked above the lockers. Weird how you notice those kinds of things when you're hiding from a psychotic secret agent.

"Come out, come out, wherever you arrrrrrre," Christmas crooned softly.

I held my tongue, keeping quiet. If I could redo *this* situation? I wouldn't have stopped running after I got into the locker room. I should've just kept going until I found another door.

"Would you just give up already?" Christmas asked. "I'm growing bored with all this running! If I wanted to run so much, I'd have joined the track team!"

"Sure," I said. "All you have to do is leave me alone and I'll stop running."

Christmas laughed. "You're in no position to negotiate. You're at the end of the line, and I think you know that too."

I heard Christmas jump. I couldn't see him, but he was probably trying to surprise me into flinching and making noise, giving away where I was hiding. Breathing slowly, I remained as still as possible.

"Look, bro," Christmas said. "Can I call you 'bro?'"

"No," I immediately answered.

He didn't care. "Bro, we got off on the wrong foot. If you'd just give me the time capsule, then maybe we can work something out. How's that sound?"

My fingers were shaking as I heard his footsteps grow closer. "What kind of deal? The same deal you made with Sophia?"

"Sophia?" Christmas asked. "If all you want is money, I can arrange that. In fact, I'll give you twenty bucks right now if you just hand it over."

"Is that how much you paid her to frame me?" I asked, even though I knew how much he paid her.

Christmas laughed. "I *wish.* She got paid a lot more to drop your wallet off and steal the capsule, plus a little extra because she did it *over* the weekend."

"But what about her now? She confessed and gave herself up," I said.

"Not my problem," Christmas replied. "She knows better than to snitch on me. If she serves time in detention, then it'll be because she stole the capsule. I won't have anything to do with that."

I felt the capsule against my back as I leaned against the lockers. Christmas's footsteps were getting closer. It was only a matter of seconds before he cornered me down the aisle. I sighed, feeling defeated. "What do you want with this capsule anyway?"

Christmas's long shadow appeared on the floor

outside the aisle. There was a good thirty seconds until he spoke again, but it felt like an eternity. "I feel like I *do* owe you an explanation since you won't be seeing daylight until you graduate. At least it'll help *me* feel better about the terrible morning you've had. Not that I *care* though."

"Thanks," I said sarcastically.

"The capsule was buried in 1999," Christmas explained. His shadow continued to creep across the cement. "It was filled with the typical boring stuff like baseball cards and newspaper clippings, but the *brainless* Principal Davis decided to include a few *extra* items. He grabbed a couple of CDs from his office and tossed them in there. I honestly think it was a mistake, but a copy of the school's computer operating system was among the discs."

"How do you know?"

"Buchanan buries and digs up a time capsule every year," Christmas said. "And Mrs. Olsen, the science teacher, keeps a list of items buried with each one."

I was confused. "But why would Principal Davis throw CDs in there?"

Christmas shrugged his shoulders. "Probably because he figured nobody would use them anymore in the future. Maybe he thought we'd open the capsule and say, '*Whoa, what are these shiny round things?*'"

"So all you want is the school's operating system?" I asked, crawling away down the aisle. "What good is *that* going to do you?"

118

Christmas laughed the kind of arrogant laugh you'd expect from a super villain. "Because I'll install it on my laptop. I'll fail *every* sixth grader at Buchanan. Every one of them! They'll *all* have to repeat the sixth grade because of it. What's more chaotic than an entire *school* of *super* sixth graders? I don't think *anyone* is gonna make fun of me after *that!*"

For a second, I thought I heard someone gasp, but ignored it because I was pretty sure we were alone in the locker room.

Hopelessness washed over me as I stared at the insane super sixth grader's shadow. Last week when Maddie and I were trying to bust Sebastian, we thought we were dealing with this exact thing. I was relieved to find out it *wasn't* that, but it's funny how the universe works sometimes. I guess it decided to deliver an uppercut to my chin, making the situation terrifyingly real.

Thanks, universe. *Thanks.*

As I crawled to the other end of the aisle, I glanced over my shoulder once more to make sure Christmas's shadow hadn't moved, but when I looked, it wasn't there. Gulping, I started my army crawl forward again, but my head bumped into something hard.

"Season's greetings," Christmas snarled.

Before I could respond, he grabbed the time capsule's strap on top of my shoulder and lifted me off the ground. As a kid who was only a year older than me, he was as strong as an ox!

When I was on my feet, he let go of the strap and pushed his foot against my stomach, slamming me into the lockers. I watched as he raised his fist.

Shutting my eyes, I braced for impact, hoping that he would punch my cheek instead of my beautiful nose. A gust of wind blasted against my face, tossing my hair around just before I heard what sounded like a heavy blanket falling to the floor.

All of a sudden a bright white light flooded my vision, swallowing the world around me. I wasn't sure what was happening, but it couldn't have been good. Don't people see white lights when they die? I wasn't in any pain, but was it possible that Christmas punched me *that* hard?

I heard Principal Davis's voice erupt in the distance. "Let him go, Christopher! Put him down this instant!"

Still scrunching my face, I cracked open an eye. The light was intense, making it impossible to see. And just as quickly as it appeared, it disappeared. The room fell dark again, but only for a second. The lights in the locker room switched on and I could see everything.

I saw the faces of all the sixth graders at Buchanan staring at me. Christmas was frozen in shock with his fist in the air, poised and ready to smash my face in.

"What?" Christmas whispered. "What is this?"

Looking to my left, I saw the locker room we had been running around in. The lockers weren't made of metal, but of painted cardboard. The floor we were standing on wasn't actually polished concrete either, but old wooden boards.

We *weren't* in the gym. We were still in the cafeteria!

The play that Brayden and the drama club were supposed to perform was about a werewolf on the football team! Of course there'd be a fake locker room as a set piece! The sound of a blanket falling was the curtain dropping. Across the room, I saw a boy standing next to a giant spotlight. Yes! The bright white light! I wasn't dead after all!

I laughed joyfully. I'd never in my life felt so happy to see the drama club.

A bit of drool fell from Christmas's lip. He was still in shock. I don't think his brain had caught up to reality yet.

"Busted," Brayden said from the side of the stage. His arms were folded and he looked unhappy. "Now get off my stage so we can put on this play!"

Principal Davis stepped onto the stage and approached us. "Christopher, you've got *a lot* of explaining to do."

"B-b-b-b-but I," Christopher mumbled.

Principal Davis's eyes bulged with anger as he pinched his fingers together. "Neh! *First*, you called me brainless. *Second*, you just admitted to everyone that *you* set it up so the time capsule was stolen. *Third*, you framed Brody for theft. *Fourth*, I don't have proof yet, but I bet you pulled the fire alarm. *Fifth*, you call yourself 'Christmas.' *Sixth*, you held Maddie prisoner... should I go on?"

Christopher hung his head and whispered, "No, sir."

Principal Davis took Christopher to the side of the stage where Coach Cooper met them. Together, they escorted the super sixth grader out of the room. The students in the cafeteria watched with wide eyes as the leader of Suckerpunch was taken away. I overheard a few kids talk about how they were glad Christopher's plan to fail everyone wasn't successful. Duh, right?

Maddie ran to the stage, hopping up in one athletic leap. She threw her arms around me for a second time that day. Can't say I didn't like it.

"Look at you," Maddie laughed as we walked backstage and out of sight from the rest of the sixth graders. "Saving the day again like it's no big deal."

Linus stepped out from behind one of the props. "Well done," he said.

I stepped in front of Maddie to protect her. "What are you doing here?" I asked, angry.

Maddie held her fist in the air. "You no good backstabbing son of a jackal!"

"Let me explain," said another student's voice.

Maddie turned, and straightened her posture. "Sir!" she said, surprised and saluting.

"It's alright," said the boy. He was shorter than me with brown hair. His brown eyes looked weary behind his thick rimmed glasses. Holding his hand out to me, he said, "The name's Jacob, but you can call me Cob. I'm the leader of Glitch."

I glanced at Maddie who nodded at me in return. Taking Cob's hand, I squeezed it tightly. "Valentine," I said. "Brody Valentine."

Cob put his hand on Linus's shoulder. "Linus was working as a double agent today, at *my* request."

"But why?" Maddie asked.

"You saw the video of Linus taking the capsule, right?" Cob asked.

Maddie and I nodded.

"Well we were there when Sophia dropped it off," Cob explained. "Since we already knew where it was, I sent Linus in to retrieve it."

Linus stepped forward. "I made a deal with one of Christmas's agents that I'd hand deliver the time capsule if I could join Suckerpunch. The agent asked Christmas, and he was gleeful about it."

"Apparently Christmas was excited at the thought of getting the capsule *plus* a Glitch agent on his team," said Cob. "In his arrogance, he let Linus right in."

"That's why I saw you talking to Christmas at the abandoned pool," Maddie whispered.

"Exactly," Linus said. "But it's also why I couldn't do anything to help you at the time. If I tried to protect you or help you escape, my cover would've been blown."

"My *mind* is blown," I joked.

"Now we know where the Suckerpunch hideout is," Cob said. "Plus Linus got a look at some of their plans for this year."

"Trust me," Linus said, folding his arms. "This *isn't* the last we've seen of them *or* Christmas."

Cob looked right into my eyes. "What d'you say?" he asked. "Can we consider you a member of Glitch?"

I tried to keep a straight face, but my smile finally snuck out. "Darn tootin'," I said, embarrassed at my lame choice of words.

Nobody laughed. They just looked at me like I was the strange one in the bunch, which I knew I was.

Maddie and Linus continued talking. I handed Cob the time capsule from my backpack. I literally felt relief at having the weight of the capsule off my shoulders. I almost asked if I could open it, but at that point in my day, I just didn't care anymore. I already knew what was inside anyway, so it didn't matter.

Before he disappeared backstage, Cob tossed my white leather wallet back to me. I caught it, actually happy to see it.

Stepping to the side of the stage, I joined Maddie and Linus. The lights in the cafeteria dimmed once again, and the room grew silent. The spotlight switched on, pointing directly at the center of the stage where Brayden was standing.

As the play started, I wondered what would've happened if I would've stayed out of the way today. Would I be in detention? Would I be safe? Would I have to repeat sixth grade next year along with everyone else? What else could I have done? If I could go back, would there be any part of it that I would've changed?

I shook my head, wondering if I made the right decisions.

The crowd laughed at a joke Brayden made on stage. Maddie and Linus laughed too. I never thanked Maddie for saving my butt for a *second* time in my life, but that was okay. Now that I was an official member of Glitch, I was certain I'd get the chance to return the favor someday.

For now, all was well within the walls of Buchanan. Christmas was busted, the stolen time capsule was returned, my name was cleared, and there was a werewolf cracking jokes onstage. I laughed, realizing how weird that sentence sounded.

Maddie glanced back at me and smiled softly, her eyes twinkling.

I returned the smile, feeling the best I'd ever felt in my life.

Nope, I finally decided. There wasn't a single thing in my day that I would've changed if I could.

Stories – what an incredible way to open one's mind to a fantastic world of adventure. It's my hope that this story has inspired you in some way, lighting a fire that maybe you didn't know you had. Keep that flame burning no matter what. It represents your sense of adventure and creativity, and that's something nobody can take from you. Thanks for reading! If you enjoyed this book, I ask that you help spread the word by sharing it or leaving an honest review!

- Marcus
m@MarcusEmerson.com

Marcus Emerson is the author of several highly imaginative children's books including the 6th Grade Ninja series, Secret Agent 6th Grader, Lunchroom Wars, and the Adventure Club Series. His goal is to create children's books that are engaging, funny, and inspirational for kids of all ages - even the adults who secretly never grew up.

Born and raised in Colorado Springs, Marcus Emerson is currently having the time of his life with his beautiful wife Anna and their three amazing children. He still dreams of becoming an astronaut someday and walking on Mars.

Made in the USA
Monee, IL
07 January 2021